LOOKING FOR DAVY JONES

A 1967 Coming-of-Age Tale

DIANA FERRARE-MAGALDI

Registration #TXu 2-067-454

CONTENTS

DEDICATION

I'd like to dedicate this book to "P" & "Bunny"… Patty Pettinelli & Glenda Knight – Resendez, my lifelong friends and soul sisters…

For all the kids in the class whom I shall never forget…

And, The Monkees, you touched our hearts through your music, talent, and positive message, it meant more than you know.

PROLOGUE

2012

"P, did you hear? Where are you? Patty? Okay, I'm hanging up; call me back." As I drive, I realize I couldn't remember where I was going. My head swirled in a thousand different directions from the news I just heard on the radio. Davy Jones: Dead at 66.

I hear his voice singing the chorus, "Cheer up Sleepy Jean," from "Daydream Believer." That song stood for everything we dreamed. I turn the volume up and just lose it. Tears stream from my eyes as my mind transports me back almost 50 years. I am shocked at my reaction. What is wrong with me?

We always had a lead. Five young teen age girls searching for Davy Jones, British singer/songwriter, a member of the band, The Monkees. Our trek through the neighborhood of Laurel Canyon in 1967 gave us hope of finding something better. We thought that if we could just find him and the band, everything would be okay.

Chapter One

KINDRED SPIRITS

1967

"Look, there it is!" Sara pointed.

"It does look like a gingerbread house!" Glenda said.

"This must be it!" Patty agreed.

We waited around for an hour hiding behind the bushes. There were several cars parked in the driveway.

"The band must be in there! Let's go closer and…" I started to say.

"Shhhh!! The front door is opening, finally!" Patty said.

We could hear footsteps approaching! Natalia had to clasp her hand over Sara's mouth as she squealed.

1966

A year earlier in 1966, seventh grade was extremely hard for me. When my family moved from Ohio I was lost. I missed all our family and friends we left behind. No one asked me how I felt before or after the move. I thought this would be easy because this was a Catholic school like the one in Ohio.

It was the first day of school. I felt ugly, fat, scared, and lonely. I was sure the ugly, navy blue uniform made my chubby body look like a box. As I walked around the school's black top during recess there was not one tree or bit of shade in sight. It was bright, hot, and I felt miserable. Where were all the trees?

My mind brought me back to Ohio. Nothing ever compared to the beauty of walking in the parkway, the long central walkway of trails that stretched for miles, on a fall day. The gold, yellow, orange, and red leaves adorned the trees and scattered the landscape like precious jewels. I loved raking the leaves up in our backyard and jumping in. I could still imagine the smell of leaves and the feel of the brisk air on my face. I had never felt more alive! It was glorious! My Dad's brother, my Uncle Gil, had just sent me pictures of the fall leaves with one Maple leaf pressed in between the pictures because he knew how much I loved them.

Too shy to approach anyone, I noticed a group of girls huddled together whispering and giving me inquisitive looks. I discovered later that their names were Ellie, Peggy, Tara, Haili, and Jenny. As they stared, I wished I could become invisible.

Then, she appeared out of nowhere. She was tall and stocky with short, brown hair fashioned with a small ponytail on top of her head. Her big, brown eyes were friendly and her smile extended ear to ear as she spoke. "Hi, I'm Patty! Do you want to play?"

"Yes, I would. My name is Diane."

We became instant friends that day. I decided to nickname her P.

Patty was a smart girl and maintained good grades. She quickly scurried about and rarely sat still except in class when she was forced to. On the weekends, whenever I wanted to get together or go to her house, Patty always had an excuse why she could not go out or have anyone over. There was always something behind that smile, a sort of sadness. She was always willing to help out on school projects, and at those times she could be funny and upbeat. Regardless, I sensed a darkness about her. I noticed how rapidly her mood could change at times and suddenly, rather than helping, she would become bossy and critical. Patty never held back. She said exactly what was on her mind at all times. I had to hand it to her. Sometimes, I wished I had the courage to be so upfront and honest.

Unlike Patty, I avoided confrontation regularly for fear of being rejected or hurting someone's feelings. Yet, as much as I secretly admired her ability to speak up, I felt angry when she would yell. I could not figure out why she acted-out like that, and wondered why?

At first it was just Patty and myself, but soon after, Natalia found us, or maybe we found her. Natalia was Sara's best friend so naturally Sara would follow.

Grade school would have been unbearable without them.

Chapter Two

THE REBELS, THE GOODIE TWO SHOES, AND THE LONER

1967

In eighth grade, two months after school started, Glenda transferred over from a public school. She came up to Patty, Natalia, Sara, and I in the school yard during recess. We were in the middle of a game of four square. Glenda was a bit shy at first and just stood there. Sara looked over and invited her to join in. She accepted and without waiting for her turn, she looked at Natalia to move aside. Natalia did not budge, so Sara stepped aside to let Glenda in. That was just like Sara, she was easy-going. Her personality was a welcome addition to our otherwise intense personalities. Sara was also incredibly bright and practical, but not as daring as the rest of us. She was kind of a "Goodie Two Shoes" who decided she would rather hang out with us rebels.

Glenda made it a point to hold her own and remained at our side after that. She was a tall girl with long legs, brown wavy hair and big brown eyes. She was incredibly bright, opinionated and uptight at times. I managed to make her laugh with my dumb jokes and then she would chill out.

We were not surprised in the least that Natalia did not move out of the square for Glenda. She was not the type of kid who would let anyone push her around. Her brown wavy hair cascaded around her beautiful face and perfectly-proportioned body. Being almost a year older than the rest of us, we never got to see her awkward stage, if she had one at all. She must have been the object of every boy's wonderment and every girl's insecurities. She was smart, funny, and very liberal in her thinking, just like her parents. They were not strict with her at all. She got to go anywhere she pleased. That's one of the reasons I liked going over to her house. My parents never suspected where we really were at times. Like the time after we won the volleyball tournament. We spent the night at Barbara Jean's house and unfortunately, got drunk. Natalia and I didn't socialize with her much after that.

Barbara Jean waited on the sidelines for her turn to play four square. Her face was stern and her posture resolute. She seemed to have two different personalities. Sometimes, she would completely fall apart and throw tantrums. At other times, she would be in control, act rigid, and disingenuous. She imagined things and would stare you down with her dark, brown eyes to intimidate you. If that did not work, she would start an argument. The boys treated her like one of the guys. She really didn't fit in any of the groups. She was a loner. I wasn't sure if that was by choice or because most of the girls were afraid of her. Natalia and I were not afraid of her because she was a terrific athlete. I was captain of our volleyball team. The three of us were unstoppable during our tournaments. I would set the ball up to Natalia, who would then set it up to Barbara Jean by the net. Because Barbara Jean had a strong, muscular body, no one on the other teams could retrieve her ferocious spike down the other side of the net. That's how we ended up winning the championship. Even though we won, the other girls on our team got upset because they hardly got their hands on the ball.

It did not take long for Ellie, Peggy, Tara, Haili, and Jenny to hear about our getting drunk. They all started to stare and whisper again. These girls were the teacher's pets — girls who came from wealthy families. They were smart, and never got into trouble. They called themselves "The Good Girls." I nicknamed them and always referred to them as "The Goodie Two Shoes." They were inseparable and mostly kept to themselves. And that was just fine with us.

But even if we wanted to keep to ourselves as well, my group and their group were destined for togetherness by the divine order of our school…St. Ambrosia.

Chapter Three

THE TACK

Our teacher's name was Sister Mary Demarian. She had to be about 75-years-old. She appeared to be tiny and frail, but nothing could be further from the truth. She was angry and frustrated most of the time, probably because the boys were relentless with their pranks that drove her certifiably insane. As we assembled in our seats after recess, I noticed something written on the bulletin board. It read: "Blessed are those who sits here shall rise!"

She did not notice the writing and sat down in her seat. With a shrill that could turn your blood cold, she screamed, "Augh!!!"

Someone had put a tack on her seat! She shot up out of her seat and immediately started going up and down the aisles screaming and pointing. "Was it you? Was it you? Was it you?"

Short and stocky, with large glasses that rimmed his piercing, dark brown eyes, Casey was the sweetest kid on the planet, but his kindness was lost on Sister. He always seemed to be her target. He was not like the other boys. He was mature, always a gentleman, and interesting. In spite of this, Sister couldn't stand the attention he directed toward her. Any other kid would be considered to be paying attention in class, but Casey seemed to goad her by staring at her with a smirk on his face.

We knew he hadn't done anything, but she unleashed her fury on him anyway. With screams and spit spewing from her twisted lips, she beat him as her habit and crucifix spun completely around her neck! She continued to punch and beat him over and over while he was already on the ground. None of us moved or could hardly breathe.

I could see the back of Preston's long neck and protruding ears turn beet red like his hair and I knew it was him. Paul was rapidly bobbing his leg up and down. He kept tapping his fingers on his desk while he stared out the window with his steely, blue eyes. Ronnie's chubby round face was buried in his arms on his desk. These actions were a sure give away of their involvement as well.

When class was dismissed, through my stunned silence I asked Casey, "Are you all right?" He just looked at me through tear-filled eyes, squeezed my hand and nodded, yes.

"Why don't you tell her you didn't do it? Why don't you speak up and defend yourself?"

With the same smirk on his face that he gave Sister, he spoke with deep conviction. "I don't want to give her the satisfaction. It makes her crazier when I just stare at her. That's why she picks on me!"

"Well then, you are asking for it!" I protested. "Idiots!" Those boys are idiots and so immature! They are always doing stupid pranks! Don't you remember when Preston and Ronnie put the rotten eggs in the wall heaters?"

"Yes, the room reeked for weeks after that," he said.

"Well, nobody thinks it's funny except for them, and as usual, you have to pay the price! Sister kept slapping your face until you admitted that you did it and you didn't!"

"I know, I know, I remember," he agreed.

"Let the other boys stand up to her and admit it. I don't want to see you hurt anymore!"

"It's okay, chill out, don't worry about me; I'm fine," he whispered. "Besides, she's after me not you, so why are you getting so upset?"

"Because when she hurts you I can feel your pain myself somehow."

"How? Why?"

"I don't know why or how, it just happens. Maybe it's because you are my friend, right?"

"Right!"

I walked away with my eyebrows raised and shaking my head. I was trying to figure out what possessed Casey to encourage these assaults. How could he be fine? It almost seemed liked he enjoyed it somehow. Or maybe he felt it was a penance for some hidden sin. I was confused by my reaction just like he was. The other kids were also upset, but not as much as me. I liked Casey, but just as a friend because he seemed a bit effeminate. Yet, I still could not figure out why it bothered me on such a deep level whenever I saw injustice or people hurt.

THE CHURCH AND SCHOOL WERE BUILT IN THE EARLY 1900s. The building already seemed pretty old in the 1960s when we attended. The ceilings were high and the windows were placed four feet from the floor to about 15-feet high. To open the windows, we had to use a 12-foot stick that had a hook on the top. All the gas heaters were attached to the wall. We had to be very careful not to get too close. The classroom itself was small with built-in lockers and closets in the back. The desks were old fashioned with wooden tops that lifted up and held our books inside.

At that point in time, Catholic school was a mixed bag of good and bad. They were run pretty much the same. Children were to be seen and not heard. We had no rights at all. We had to be obedient because if you weren't, you would get the crap beaten out of you. There was no running to our parents because they would simply back up the teachers. It was believed that discipline was needed to raise children to become responsible adults. When it was not done right, the children pay the price.

The Priests and Nuns could be brutal at times with either their beatings or humiliating comments. In order to survive, we joked around a lot to make each other laugh. The laughter was a vain attempt — a release to cover up the anxiety we felt from our uncertain surroundings. None of us knew who would be smacked next. It was better to laugh than to cry.

This was our last year in this school. We were now the big, eighth graders that all the younger kids looked up to. Patty and I sat side by side next to each other. The problem was when one of us would start to laugh, or when I saw her shoulders bob up and down, we would get hysterical and could not stop laughing! The more we tried to hide our laughter from the nuns, the worse it got. We would hide under our wooden desks until the tops would come crashing down on our heads from Sister's fists!

As the boys continued to antagonize Sister with all their stupid pranks, I started to feel sorry for her. My sympathy ended for her when she locked Casey in the closet in the back of the classroom one day for mimicking Tara during our language lessons. He was not the only one who got punished; I got in trouble too, but never the "Goodie Two Shoes!"

Tara had just finished reading one of her written stories to us for extra credit. She was talkative and an amazing storyteller for her age. I secretly admired her. I wished I had the ability to write stories and share them in class, but never had the courage to do it. She was actually very pretty, but her tall, thin body gave her an awkward appearance.

When Sister walked back from the closet where she had just put Casey, to the front of the classroom, she announced, "Okay class, I need three volunteers to diagram sentences with linking verbs on the board."

Ellie was shy and quiet, except in the classroom. Her hand was always the first to go up so she could tell us the right answers and today was no exception. Her pretty, hazel eyes never saw a lick of make-up. She kept her short hair tightly pulled back with a headband. Her diagram was perfect as usual.

Peggy followed her up to the board next. She was incredibly articulate and used words we had not learned yet. She was soft spoken, very mature, and responsible. She had straight, shoulder length blonde hair and was a bit over-weight. Peggy sat on my left, one aisle over and one seat up from my desk. I wanted to ask her for help with the school work because she was a straight A student. Instead of doing so, I chose to copy her work during tests. That was obviously not a good choice and very difficult because she kept her answers covered up most of the time.

Both girls quickly did a beautiful job on the board diagramming the sentences with ease. I was smart, but did not realize it at the time that I had a learning disability called dyslexia. It made it hard to read and as a result, my comprehension was almost non-existent. I also did not understand the basics of math. The numbers kept getting mixed up when I looked at them. I kept my eyes downcast as Sister perused the room for the next student to go up to the board.

To my horror, she called me up to the board to diagram the third sentence. This was my worst nightmare. Not only did I not understand how to do it, I would cease to breathe from the anxiety of being in front of the class!

I slowly walked up to the front and faced the board. I started to write a word, but then quickly erased it with my sweaty fingers. You could see the perspiration on the board as the chalk started to disintegrate before my eyes. I froze!

"Go on now, start doing the diagram," Sister said impatiently.

When I did not proceed to write on the board, she insisted, "You are just being defiant!"

Then, she hit the top of my hand so hard that it left a bruised imprint of her bony fingers. Now I knew how poor Casey felt. I ran out of the room and wanted to run home, but knew I would get in more trouble if I did. So, I sat in the hall on the steps and cried until she came out and got me. When I walked back into the classroom I did not know if I was more relieved that no one stared at me or if it was because Casey was out of the closet and sitting at his desk.

I SANG IN THE CHOIR WITH ALL THE OTHER GIRLS IN our class. We performed our worship hymns every Sunday for Mass. That was the only time we could wear our colorful outfits with our lace Mantilla's upon our heads. We liked parading our stylish couture. As we made our descent down the stairs to receive Holy Communion, the noise from our shoes would deafen the congregation. As we approached the Altar to receive

Holy Communion we knelt down. Robert stood next to the Priest. He was one of the Altar Boys who held the gold communion plate under our chin in case the Consecrated Host fell to the ground. I was about to swallow it when he leaned over and whispered in my ear, "You girls sound like a herd of cows!"

"Shut up, smarty pants!" I hissed.

Patty was kneeling next to me when she decided to reach through the Altar rail and grab the bottom of Robert's vestment alb. That's the black gown the Altar Boys wore that was always too long to begin with. It made him trip and fall. She had seen the boys in our class do this to the Altar Boys on countless occasions and thought this would be a good time to give Robert a dose of his own medicine. Father Francis was furious as he helped him to his feet. Patty and I got up fast and walked back down the aisle in the opposite direction keeping our heads down to hide our laughter.

Robert reminded me of Clark Kent. He was a handsome boy with brown hair and wore big glasses. He was smart, responsible, and articulate, but sometimes to a fault. I liked him, but he never missed an opportunity to throw a sarcastic zinger at me, or anyone else for that matter. I didn't like it when he did that to me and thought it was because he didn't like me.

Once Robert was back on his feet, Father Francis continued to administer Holy Communion. Casey stood on the other side of the Priest still holding the bells. He was the Server and required to perform this task with reverence and dignity. During the Mass it was his job to pour the water on the priest's hands to purify them.

Casey seemed unsteady and most of the water went on the floor. After the consecration of the bread and wine, the Altar Boy is supposed to ring the bells to signal what was to happen next. He kept ringing the bells at the wrong times and mumbled the Latin prayers because he could not remember them. Once again, we were all laughing because we knew why he was messing it all up. Apparently, he had enjoyed quite a few sips of wine before Mass. It was not uncommon for the boys to sneak a sip or two. Obviously, Casey had too many sips! He also didn't know that the wine was actually Father Francis' scotch that he drank. It was a good thing he sent Casey home after Mass before Sister discovered both of their secrets.

I really enjoyed singing the hymns because it made me feel closer to God. One day, I unfortunately showed up late to choir practice. The choir director, Sister Mary Alman, punched me really hard in the breast. The pain went so deep on so many levels. I quit the choir after that.

These people were supposed to be Godly examples for us. We were young and impressionable. Yes, we goofed off, but none of us ever talked back or were disrespectful. I know all the kids drove the nuns crazy at times. But, we did not deserve to be spanked, punched, verbally abused, or humiliated. How were we supposed to have a relationship with God and understand His forgiveness and love when the people representing Him could be so awful at times? Where was Saint Theresa? She was the Patron Saint I chose for my Confirmation a few years earlier. Saint Theresa of Lisieux was a

Carmelite nun called the "Little Flower." She was only 24-years-old when she died in 1897. She was the perfect example of the gospel paradox that we gain our life by losing it when God draws us out of ourselves to serve others. She said, "Our Lord does not look so much at the greatness of our actions or even at their difficulty as at the love with which we do them." I was sure there were Priests and Nuns somewhere out there who were like her, so I never gave up hope that someday one would appear.

Chapter Four

FIRST KISS

The next day during recess, I was sitting on the old log that separated the small flower bed and the hot pavement. That is where Patty, Glenda, Sara, Natalia and I usually congregated to sit and chat after we played. With my elbows on my knees and hands on my cheeks, I held up my head. I could see the other girls across the yard staring again. There were lots of kids in our class, but the ones who stood out to me were the five girls, "The Goodie Two Shoes." I was a little jealous of them because they were smart and I felt dumb. To cover up my insecurity I became loud and to my surprise, popular. In spite of that, they hardly spoke to me and just kept staring and whispering.

Natalia noticed how quiet I was and asked, "What's wrong with you? Why did you quit the choir?"

"Oh, you were not there when Sister punched Diane," Glenda replied.

"Don't let that stop you from being with us!" Sara said.

"That's right, come on now, let it go!" Patty encouraged.

"Maybe, I'll think about it," I reluctantly responded. As I looked up, I could see the other girls across the yard still staring. "Why do they always seem to be staring at me?

"For Pete's sake Diane, not everything is about you!" Natalia snapped.

Patty quickly came to my defense. "No, No! They do stare at her. I think it is because they think she is a bad girl."

"Why?" Glenda asked eagerly awaiting my reply.

I put my head in my hands again and covered my eyes as I replied. "Glenda, you were not here last year so you don't know about Greg."

"Who is that?" she asked.

"I think I got my bad reputation for dating Greg, an eighth grade boy last year when I was in the seventh grade.

The girls now surrounded me, glued to my every word.

"His name was Greg. He was my Steve McQueen! He was a handsome athlete with platinum blond hair, sparkling blue eyes, and big full beautiful lips! He was so sweet to me and carried my books as he walked me home almost every day! One day, he hesitantly asked, "Will you be my girlfriend?"

Naturally, I agreed. "Wow! Yes, of course!" I told him.

I couldn't believe I actually had a boyfriend! Then he asked, "Would you like to go with me to my eighth grade graduation swim party?"

"Well…um…yes…okay…I would love to," I reluctantly agreed.

"First of all, being in a bikini has never been a comfortable choice for me. As you guys know, I am a little chubby and have huge breasts for my age. I was embarrassed to show my body. I figured I would just keep the towel on and not go in the pool. We went to Ronnie and Mary Anne's house. They have a beautiful home in the Hollywood Hills and a very handsome Father."

"Oh, I know!" Patty giggled.

"Anyway," I continued, "The eighth grade girls were less than pleased that a seventh grader had been invited to the party. The first thing Mary Anne did when she saw me was rip off my towel. I thought I was going to die!"

"Later that night after dinner, the slow dancing started. We started to dance to "Chances Are" by Johnnie Mathis. It was the most wondrous moment and then, he kissed me! My first kiss! I kissed him back. It was then and there I realized that neither one of us should have eaten the spicy, onion flavored chili!"

"Eyew!!!" the girls all said at once.

As we all started to laugh, I continued my story.

"The next day at school it was like the Spanish Inquisition. The nuns caught wind there had been a party. That was not allowed and whoever attended was in big, big trouble! I guess boys like to exaggerate what really happened. That's how I got my bad reputation and why Greg's mother made him break up with me!"

"Wow!" Glenda said. "That's still kind of romantic in a weird sort of way."

"Don't give those girls another thought," Patty declared.

Natalia chimed in and said, "Who cares what they think anyway!"

"Yeah!" Sara agreed.

As we headed back to our classroom, Glenda turned and reminded us, "Don't forget about tomorrow. Be at my house no later than 2 p.m!"

Chapter Five

LAUREL CANYON AND THE BANDS

Laurel Canyon in the Hollywood Hills had a life of its own. It was right around the corner from Hollywood Boulevard and near the Sunset Strip. When you turned the corner from the city lights, you magically found yourself in a rustic neighborhood. The narrow streets had no sidewalks with cars lined up and down for miles. It was a mix between the Old West and Sherwood Forest. It was enchanting and I loved it.

It was Saturday afternoon and all our chores were done finally. With our thumbs out, Patty, Natalia, and I made our way to Glenda's house in Laurel Canyon. Sara was already there. Being very tall and thin she appeared a bit awkward. We could always count on Sara to be our navigator on Look Out Mountain in The Canyon as we searched for celebrities. She always had her transistor radio so we could listen to all the pop hits and B-Bop up and down the streets. We always enjoyed our adventures together.

When we arrived at Glenda's house, she seemed upset, but did not say why. Sara told us that she just found out that Micky Dolenz and Peter Tork lived somewhere in the Canyon. You can't imagine our excitement as we scoured the winding streets that always smelled like pine and pot.

We made our usual stop at the Laurel Canyon Country Store. This is where all the so called "hippies" hung out. This area was considered L.A.'s Haight-Ashbury. It was a melting pot of young people with colorful outfits, beads, and feathers. Little did we know at the time that some of those crazy, friendly people were already, or about to become, the legends of Rock and Roll. They were the best singer/song writers and musicians of our generation. When the Mamas and the Papas came out with their song, "Twelve Thirty," and sung about "Young Girls of the Canyon," I was convinced that they must have been writing it about us!

Carol King, one of my favorites, lived and wrote "Tapestry" there. Jim Morrison's song, "Love Street," was inspired by the Canyon. Micky Dolenz, Peter Tork, Buffalo Springfield, The Eagles, The Mamas and The Papas, Crosby Stills & Nash, Linda Ronstadt, and Joni Mitchell, just to name a few, all lived or visited there.

Our solitary mission was to find The Monkees: Davy Jones, Micky Dolenz, Michael Nesmith, and Peter Tork. The band originated in 1965 and became an unexpected sensation when their television show, "The Monkees," made its debut in September of 1967 and ran for two seasons. It was inspired by the The Beatles' "Hard Day's Night" movie.

With their Marx Brothers humor and insane boyish charms, these four actor/musicians won the hearts of "The Young Generation" and they certainly won our hearts! It was our favorite television show. It was said that in 1967, they sold more records than The Beatles and The Rolling Stones combined. They were one of the most successful bands of the 1960s and sold approximately 75 million records or more worldwide to date. The only thing better than listening to The Monkees was listening as a group during one of our regular sleepovers.

Chapter Six

THE PAJAMA PARTY

Glenda was a perfectionist about everything. Her room was spotless and beautifully decorated. I loved her big, but cozy canopy bed. There were several large bedroom windows that looked like paintings. The view of the trees and hills were magical.

Her mom used to be a ballerina and was very petite, pretty, warm, and friendly. Her dad was a grip at the Hollywood studios and earned a good living. He was tall and handsome. They were both very hospitable and generous. We always enjoyed and usually stayed overnight at their home on Ridpath Drive in Laurel Canyon. Our slumber parties consisted of eating them out of house and home, and skinny-dipping at night in their pool. This was our happy place, our sanctuary and escape from our realities and problems we had in our home life. Unfortunately, and unbeknownst to us, Glenda's home life was not as perfect as we thought.

Earlier that day, before we arrived at Glenda's house,

she found herself yet again sitting on the stairs in the hallway next to her little brother who was covering his ears. They were waiting in silence for their parents to stop arguing.

Glenda's mother was seated at the kitchen table crying out of frustration as she stammered, "If you want our marriage to work, you have to stop enabling Yolanda."

"I have asked you over and over again, how can I turn my back on my daughter?" he yelled.

"She is 25-years-old and completely dependent on you. She doesn't even have a job, nor does she make any effort to do so. If you keep bailing her out, she will never stand on her own two feet."

"I'm sorry, but I will always help her no matter what!" he insisted.

"Don't you get it? You are not helping her; you are crippling her!"

"Stop, just stop!" Glenda blurted out as she emerged from the stairwell into the kitchen. "My friends will be here any minute!"

Glenda had to hear this same argument almost every day except for the days and weeks her mother gave her father the silent treatment. The solution was nowhere in sight and nothing ever changed.

That evening in Glenda's bedroom, we were all tired and a little crabby. We had been in the hot sun all day searching the Canyon and it was still muggy outside. Patty started to nitpick at Natalia. She was annoyed because Natalia rushed us through the neighborhoods. She was not as interested or invested in our quest to find the band as the rest of us. When Patty started to complain, Natalia was not having it and rolled her large, hazel-green eyes. As a result, they began to bicker. I was getting on Glenda's nerves because I was already planning our itinerary for the next day.

Sara was an only child and very mature for her age. She usually did not create a lot of drama. For some reason that evening, she seemed agitated and angry. She had been submerged in her thoughts about the argument she had with her mother earlier that morning. "Momma, Momma! Can't you hear me? Please get off the telephone; it's been over two hours!" Her mother was on an overseas call to her sister in Hungary. She was always on the phone. She ignored Sara as usual.

Her father was sitting in the living room in front of the television in his favorite chair. You could always find him in that spot. Turning to her father, Sara pleaded, "Papa, I need to call Natalia; it's important! But her father just kept smoking his pipe and reading his newspaper. He barely looked up, and when he did, he said nothing.

Sara dared to raise her voice and shouted, "I need to use the phone!!!" Her mother abruptly stopped her conversation with her sister on the telephone and turned toward Sara. She sternly replied in her native Hungarian language, "Be patient you silly girl or you will not be allowed to go out today!"

Natalia noticed that Sara was far away and biting her lower lip. She knew Sara well enough to know that she was upset. Natalia did not have any more patience for Sara than her parents did. Soon, Natalia's annoyance showed itself when she blurted out, "What's your problem?"

As Sara's green eyes started to tear up, she turned toward the rest of us, burst into tears, and replied, "Natalia and I used to be best friends. But ever since you guys came into the picture, she doesn't have time for me anymore!"

Chapter Seven

CONFESSIONS

"What the hell are you talking about? Most of us have been together for over a year! Besides, I'm right here!" Natalia yelled.

Glenda rolled her eyes while Patty paced back and forth. I put my arm around Sara. "Look at it this way, Sara, you now have four best friends!"

Patty finally sat down and joined our circle on the floor as we reassured and comforted Sara with hugs and tissues.

Sara's vulnerable confession inspired all of us to open up. Glenda got up and peeked out of her bedroom door into the hallway. She quietly shut the door and sat back down. Holding back her tears she whispered.

"My parents live in the same house, but not as husband and wife. My poor dad has to sleep downstairs in the basement because my mom can't stand Yolanda, my half-sister. In a way, I see my mom's point. Yolanda is always creating a crisis or needs money and my dad always runs to her rescue! Mom refuses to accept it and resents dad for putting Yolanda first instead of us!"

We were all amazed and disillusioned because we thought they were the perfect couple, unlike the rest of our parents.

Natalia looked around, hesitated a moment, and quickly said, "Well at least your dad treats you like his little girl. My Popi continually tells me about his problems with my mother. He told me once that there's no longer any passion with each other because she is frigid and boring. My mom told me she thinks he is having an affair, but she never says anything to him! She also told me she is the last person in her home that he considers. My grandmother is the first person he greets when he comes home, then me, and then my little sister. I feel sorry for my mom, but I don't like being put in the middle when they complain to me behind each other's back. I feel like I have to be the parent!"

This intimate information about her parents' love life was uncomfortable and embarrassing to hear. But, we were friends and wanted to show our support so we listened even though she did not seem to need consoling. Natalia never cried, or so we thought.

For as long as Natalia could remember, her father and grandmother would tell her stories about Juan and Eva Peron. His first term as the president of Argentina was from 1946 to 1955. They wanted to eliminate poverty and dignify the laborer. Evita became very

powerful within the pr
for labor rights. Sh
suffrage movement
female Peronist p

Natalia nev
ten-years-old
er's stories a
support for
Eva Peron.

Natalia abruptly got up
the door. Her Father immediately
are you going? Come back here."

Natalia stomped her foot and started to
Popi, I have heard it a hundred times. I want to go
and play!

"Stop crying! It is important that you know and understand the history of your native country. You must learn how to fight for a good cause and take what you want. You must be strong, not weak like your mother! Always remember, never cry!"

Chapter Eight

THE OTHER DAUGHTER

I took my eyes off Natalia and gathered my courage to speak up and finally confessed, "I just want to be with you guys. At home I feel invisible. I almost jumped off the balcony when we first moved here to California, but then my dog, Bridgette, started barking."

"Why would you do that?" Glenda replied.

"I missed everyone from back home in Cleveland. Here in California, people are only interested in Cindy, my sister, and her career."

Cindy is a model and is making a movie right now. My entire family went to the beach on location to watch her take the publicity photographs. This was the first time I attended a movie production. It was exciting and I felt proud of Cindy. She looked so beautiful. I had no idea how well she could act and dance. Both my parents went to her photo shoots and filming every chance they got. When my father couldn't go, my mom had one of her friends take her.

At one point during the shoot I asked, "Mom, can you and Pop come to my volleyball tournament?"

"Volleyball?"

"Yes, remember, I'm the captain of the team?"

"You are? Oh, I didn't know that."

"Yes you do, I told you about it. Remember you washed my uniform?"

"No, I don't remember."

"Well, can you come?"

"You know we both work in the afternoons and besides your father can't get off work to drive me."

Just then, one of the cast members came over to greet my parents. He turned to me and said, "Oh, you're the sister."

My mom responded and said, "Yes, this is my other daughter."

Ever since then, everywhere I go, people always say, "Oh, you're the sister," and when my mom introduces me, she still says, "This is my other daughter."

AFTER RECALLING THAT HORRIBLE DAY, I COULD NOT stop the tears from flowing. I sobbed loudly before asking rhetorically, "Other than what? Really? Other daughter?" I exclaimed. "Did she forget my name? You guys are the only ones who don't ask me a thousand questions about my sister."

"Well, we see you Diane," Glenda assured me. "And, we'll never forget your name."

"Yeah!" Sara replied.

"Don't feel so bad about the volleyball games; you are not the only one who has parents who never show up," Natalia confessed.

At this point, we all stared at Patty, eager to hear her story. She knew what we were thinking and shot up from the floor and went straight to Glenda's record player. She chose to play "Day Dream Believer." She sat back down on the floor and closed her eyes when she heard Davy's voice singing "Cheer up Sleepy Jean."

"What's wrong? I asked.

"Nothing, nothing is wrong."

"Come on P, I know you. You always play that song when you're upset."

"No I don't; I just felt like hearing it. That doesn't mean there is anything wrong!"

We were all staring at her in silence. She knew we didn't buy her story.

At first, Patty's eyes looked like huge saucers. I did not think she was going to open up. But then, her eyes narrowed, her lips tightened and then she hissed, "I hate my mother; she is a witch!"

Chapter Nine

CHOICES

We did not move a muscle as we waited for Patty to elaborate. "My mom beats my sister, my brother, and me! She says horrible things to us and we have to stay in our rooms most of the time like prison! If it weren't for my dad, I would never get to go out of the house! And, and...," she hesitated as she clenched her fist, put her head down and wiped a tear from her eye.

Sara put her hand on Patty's arm. "What is it?"

"She just kicked my sister, Laura, out of the house!" Patty answered.

"Why, what for?" Glenda whispered.

"She is pregnant! My mom is a nurse and she arranged for Laura to have an abortion!"

"Oh my God, did she do it?" I asked.

"When Laura decided to have the baby, my mom lost her mind! So, my dad helped Laura find an apartment and now my mom won't speak to any of us!"

Patty took a deep breath, sighed, and then declared, "I'm never having kids!"

Yikes! Her story was far worse that any of ours. It made me appreciate my family because I did enjoy some good times with them especially when they entertained friends and family. There was always good food and laughter. Patty never had that.

Natalia shook her head in agreement. "Well, maybe your sister should have an abortion; she is too young to take care of a baby anyway."

"Are you kidding me?" She could give the baby up for adoption! There are so many people who would love to adopt a baby and give them a good, loving home," I protested.

"No!" Natalia continued, "she should be free to decide what she wants for her life! Besides, it's her body!"

Shaking my head in disbelief, I questioned, "What about the baby's body? The mother's body is the one place a baby should be safe, not destroyed! It's a human being! I have heard stories about how dangerous it can be for the mother and also how in some cases, it haunts them for the rest of their life!"

As Sara nodded in agreement with me, she asked Natalia, "Where do you get such ideas?"

Natalia answered. "My family and I are from South America. Like Europe, we are much more liberal and sophisticated in our views than Americans."

"Oh really, is that what you want to call it? You know what? Let's not talk about this anymore. It is literally making me feel sick!" I replied.

"Shush!" Glenda interrupted. "My parents will hear you, keep your voices down! Listen, I guess there are certain views that we are not always going to agree on. Diane is right. Let's avoid those subjects and agree to disagree. Otherwise, we will be fighting all the time instead of supporting one another."

Support is what we all needed. As young, teenage girls, everything was new and exciting, but at the same time frightening and confusing.

Chapter Ten

SOUL SISTERS

We were just starting to figure it all out and discovering not just our own views, but each other's as well. Even though we argued and disagreed at times, it was okay in the end because it kept all of us in check and on our toes.

Before that night no one knew the insecurity and pain we carried inside. We did our best to hide it from our classmates and each other. Now that we confided in one another, it was amazing. An unbreakable bond of soul sisters was born. What I longed for in my sister was discovered in my friends. It was a collective knowing and understanding. To give and receive this kind of acceptance and love was spiritual and would remain a part of each other's lives well into the future. We were no longer alone. The friends you make as children have a deeper impact on one's life, than those made later. It's a family member that you choose.

We dried our eyes and ate like there was no tomorrow. Glenda's mom always cooked for us. Her homemade fried chicken and french fries were a personal favorite. Glenda's dad would make his famous Mexican dishes. The homemade tamales, tacos, guacamole, salsa, and tortilla chips were also my favorite. They also had an endless supply of cookies, plenty of ice cream, candy, and soda pop.

Best of all, Glenda's mom was never uptight about us being out at night. We all needed a break from the heaviness of our previous confessions and asked if she would drive us to Sunset and Vine. Whether it was because she wanted time on her own, trusted us, or was completely oblivious to the dangers of teenage girls being alone at night, she agreed and twenty minutes later, we entered the famed Wallichs Music City.

Wallichs Music City was the first great record store in Hollywood. We lost all track of time as we perused the aisles. There was so much to look at and buy. They had musical instruments, sheet music, concert tickets, LPs and 45s. One of the best features in this record store were the soundproof listening stations. They looked like tiny, wooden telephone booths with large, glass windows that could fit one, maybe two persons at a time. This was where you could listen to the record before you bought it. I purchased my first Monkees Album, aptly titled, "The Monkees."

"The Last Train to Clarksville" was my favorite song on the album. Patty bought "The Monkees" album as well. "Day Dream Believer" and "I'll Be True To You" were her favorites. She was so in love with Davy that I thought her heart would burst.

There were many records and albums from other artists that we collected as well. Sara was a talented piano player. She bought the sheet music and 45 record to "California Dreamin" from The Mamas and The Papas. Natalia bought "White Rabbit" from Jefferson Airplane and spent the entire time flirting with the guys at the register.

GLENDA'S MOM WAS WAITING PATIENTLY FOR US IN THE parking lot, just as she promised. She never complained about how long we had been in there. She probably enjoyed the solitude while smoking the one cigarette she looked forward to and snuck at the end of the day. We piled into the car and headed home, excited about our purchases.

When we returned to Glenda's house, we listened to our new records while we danced and sang along. Glenda's favorite Monkees song was "I Wanna Be Free," but that night, she played the 45 record she had just purchased called "Hurt So Bad" from "Little Anthony and The Imperials," over and over, while she cried for a boy in our class, who she claimed was the love of her life. He was a really cute boy named Frank, but he hardly looked at her. He might have been shy, but Glenda thought he just was not interested. She did not have the courage to go up to him first.

After the inevitable pillow fight, we made our way to the pool. We dove in with reckless abandon and enjoyed the sensation of the crisp cool water on our naked bodies. At the time, I thought it was the most exhilarating moment of my life.

Glenda was the only one who did not dive into the pool. She was finicky about her long, brown hair and did not want it to frizz up. While we swam, she never got off the raft. She even wore a shower cap that made her ears stick out, so Patty nicknamed her "Bunny."

Chapter Eleven

WONDERLAND

It was a beautiful and sunny Sunday morning. When we woke up, we decided it was a perfect day to search the Canyon again. Before we started our trek, everyone was scattered and getting ready. I wanted one more dip in the pool, so I grabbed my bathing suit and an inner tube and floated weightlessly while listening to "A Whiter Shade of Pale." It was so peaceful; both my eyes were blissfully closed. Then I heard something and noticed Glenda's dad. He came out to collect the leaves out of the pool. I stared at him with one eye barely open, hoping he would not notice.

He looked so handsome with his bronzed muscular body, long legs, and white shorts. I closed my eyes again and soon realized that he was in the pool. He quietly swam over, held me in his arms and swirled me around in the water. Suddenly, I heard Patty's voice in the background anxiously calling for me.

"Diane! Diane! Where are you?"

I opened my eyes and quickly realized I was still in the inner tube. Glenda's dad had not moved from the spot I saw him last and was still raking up the leaves. I realized that what I just experienced was all in my mind. It was all just a daydream, a fantasy.

What was wrong with me? I wondered why the hell I was even thinking that! There was this weird sense of awakening in me that I could not understand. I remembered that this was not the first time I had been attracted to older men. James Garner's face was dreamy; Charles Bronson was captivating; and, oh my, Paul Newman's blue eyes!

WITH HEAVY EYELINER MAKEUP IN STYLE, GLENDA would do her eyes with perfection. Before we would go on our next adventure in the Canyon, we would have to wait a lifetime while she applied and reapplied her eyeliner. For some reason, her left eye would have to be done over and over. No amount of resistance and teasing from us would derail her from her task! She never went out without her makeup.

Patty grew impatient as usual, and yelled from the porch, "Come on, Bunny! For Pete's sake, let's go! It's getting late!"

"Just one more minute, Patty; I'm almost done," Glenda replied nervously.

"You look fine, Princess!" Patty yelled again.

Throwing her makeup down on her vanity desk, Glenda angrily replied, "Jeez!"

Finally, we were off. As Sara sorted through her maps, she announced, "Hey guys, guess what? I am pretty sure that David McCallum lives in these hills as well."

"Oh my gosh! are you kidding me? 'The Man from U.N.C.L.E.' is one of my favorite shows! I have a huge crush on David McCallum. He plays Illya Kuryakin!"

"Diane, you have a crush on everyone!" Natalia sarcastically replied through gritted teeth.

"No! No!" Patty shook her head. "We don't have enough time today to look for him too!"

"Yeah," Glenda agreed. "Remember, we have to stop by Eric's house. He said his band knows where Micky Dolenz lives."

With a smile on her face, Sara nudged Glenda on the side with her elbow. "You just want to go back there again because he's a cute 17-year-old and in a band."

"Hey Glenda, what's the band's name again?" I asked.

"Iron Butterfly," she replied.

"I remember now," I said. "We went there a couple of months ago. What was the name of that song they were working on? It sounded something like Innaga-gadadavidadada?" The music was too loud. I didn't like it.

When we arrived at Eric's house, we waited outside while Glenda went in to get the address. After a few minutes, when she emerged with a huge smile on her face, we knew we hit the jackpot! Waving a piece of paper in the air way up over her head she shouted, "Wonderland! he lives on Wonderland!"

It was a long hike as we climbed up hills and over walls. We never noticed our scratched elbows and knees. Everything I knew about The Monkees was ruminating in my head. The Monkees were on TV on Monday nights. I never missed it. I liked all of them. Micky Dolenz was definitely my favorite. He was the funniest! I thought his voice was the best and he could play the drums as well. Peter was adorably childlike and I loved his blond hair! Michael was clearly a great musician and talented song writer. And then there was Davy, cutest Brit on the planet! I loved his dimples and his little sideway shuffles when he sang and danced!

We followed the directions and walked up a really steep hill on Wonderland. We didn't have the exact address, but the note said to look for a Gingerbread house. We went as far up the street as we could.

"Look, there it is!" Sara pointed.

"It does look like a Gingerbread house!" Glenda said.

"This must be it!" Patty agreed.

We waited around for an hour hiding behind the fence and bushes. The gate was open and at least 30 feet from the front door. There were several cars parked in the driveway.

"The band must be in there! Let's go closer and…" I started to say.

"Shhhh!! the front door is opening, finally!" Patty said.

We could hear footsteps coming closer! Natalia had to clasp her hand over Sara's mouth as she squealed.

We peeked through the bushes and saw three pretty

girls and two long-haired guys emerge from the front door. They were much older than us. They turned around back toward the door saying their goodbyes, hugging and kissing whoever was standing on the other side of the doorway. Standing on our tippy toes, all we could see were the tops of the heads of the people inside the house. One had brown, curly hair and the other was blond.

As we kept pushing each other aside, we all spoke at the same time.

"That's Micky!"

"That's got to be Peter!"

"We can't see Davy; he's too short!"

"Do you think Mike's in there?"

"Do you think that's really them?"

"Shhhh!!! They will hear us!"

Then the door closed. The two long-haired guys and three pretty girls got into their Volkswagon Van. It was beautifully painted with huge colorful flowers, rainbows, hearts, and peace signs. As they drove down the driveway, their wheels screeched as they abruptly stopped. One of the girls leaned out of the car window and sarcastically asked, "Say, what are YOU girls doing here?"

I made up some BS story and replied, "We were just walking by and had to come up here to hide because these creepy guys were following us in their car."

I don't think they bought it.

"Well, YOU are NOT supposed to be here, so beat it!" she replied.

As they drove away, Sara stuck her tongue out at

them. Then we high-tailed it out of there and headed back to Glenda's.

That was the closest we had ever gotten so far. We all went home that night knowing we would see each other on Monday morning. We were certain the band had to be in there. We also knew we were going to try again and that gave us a sense of purpose.

Chapter Twelve

HUMBLE BEGINNINGS

My father was a very handsome man from Italian descent. He looked like Rock Hudson, but even more handsome. I would sit and listen to his stories about his experiences in the war over and over. I had a feeling that he only told me about the good experiences because sometimes in the middle of his stories his face would become pale as he stared into space. At times, he seemed anxious and nervous. The one story that stood out to me was when he was in a fox hole with another soldier. When the soldier was wounded my Dad tried to save him, but the soldier died. As my Dad lay there, trapped all night, he said he heard a voice tell him that he would survive. He would always say, "Jesus knows me."

He joined the army in 1942 and was honorably discharged in 1946 as a T5 corporal. Dad was with the Fighting 69th where he volunteered to be a medic. When his unit landed in Italy, they participated in the invasion of Anzio. From there, they went on to fight in the battle for Mount Casino.

After the war, my father met my mother when he was stationed in Pisa during a dance. She was a classic beauty born in Italy. She had a voluptuous body, brown hair and large, almond eyes. It took a platoon of several MPs to escort my Nonny out of the building so he could ask my mother to dance. They fell in love, got married, and settled in Cleveland where my father was born. I loved our life in Ohio.

We were not monetarily rich, but we were always well fed and dressed. Like most mothers in the 1950s and 1960s, mom sewed dresses for me and my dolls. She always wore yellow gloves as she cleaned our already spotless house including the garage floor. She ironed all of our clothes and even the sheets. We loved her cooking and hospitality as did anyone else who sat at her table.

Mom did not have any siblings so her friends became her siblings. They were a strong, collective sisterhood of war brides that became our big, Italian family. I think that is why when I made friends, I considered them my family as well. Those days, growing up in Cleveland were the happiest times for me.

We moved to Los Angeles in 1964, where we rented a two-bedroom apartment on the second story. On the first day, my mother walked out onto the balcony and shouted to the Hollywood Hills, "Population, we are going to be famous!" She was determined to make my sister a star and eventually succeeded. I wondered if that is what my sister really wanted. She loved to cook and like me, enjoyed eating. It must have been hard for her to keep a slim figure for her modeling jobs. Her beautiful, blue eyes and long, blonde hair made her absolutely breathtaking.

The studio was grooming her along with several other young actors. Tom Selleck was one of them. He took her for a ride on his motorcycle. Gosh, was he gorgeous! She went to high school at the studios, and as a result, she was hardly ever home. When she was home we did not communicate very much. She always seemed preoccupied or in a hurry to do something else. We grew up around each other, not with each other. I was in awe of her and very proud of her. I was happy for her success, but at the same time, craved my mother's attention that was lost on me.

The three of us kids had to share a room. The only time I minded it was when my brother insisted that we keep the light on at night. Sometimes things would get a bit riled up between my siblings. Gino was traumatized one time when Cindy locked him in a storage bin just to tease him. I heard of other older siblings doing crazy stunts to their little brothers or sisters, but I just could not relate.

After all, Gino was a cute kid and exceptionally smart. But because the entire focus in our household was continually on our older sister, Cindy, Gino usually kept to himself. He and I had something in common — feeling neglected at home — but never talked about it. He was a sweet, kind-hearted boy, but would lose his temper when he was provoked by Cindy. For some reason, she would antagonize him and then all hell would break loose. As the middle child, I always rescued him and tried to make peace between them. This role never ceased.

Sometimes when I got home from school, I would find him in my room playing my Monkee records. He would pretend he was playing my guitar and singing in front of an audience, until he actually taught himself to play. He started practicing every day until one day he amazed all of us when he almost flawlessly played "Mary Mary" by Michael Nesmith.

There was a six year age difference between the two of us, but I never kicked him out of my room or took the guitar away. We got along well and enjoyed watching "Lost in Space" on our tiny black and white TV. We would sit and trumpet the theme song with our mouths, and we were actually quite good.

We came from humble beginnings. My parents struggled and worked hard to send us to private school. Dad was a meat cutter and mom was a waitress. She entered the world of retail and worked her way up to manager.

Sunday nights were always bitter sweet. I enjoyed spending time with my family. We had a black and white TV that had the tiniest screen and constantly needed the rabbit ears adjusted. They were covered with aluminum foil in an attempt to receive good reception, which seemed to do the trick most of the time.

Ed Sullivan was everyone's favorite host and variety show. I learned to imitate all the regular characters. My favorite was Topo-Gigio, the lovable mouse and the little voice in the box that would say, 'Soright? Soright!' when they opened the lid. Every band, singer, musician, comedian, and acrobat made their debut on that show. I would be so excited when the show started and sad when it ended, indicating that the weekend was over, and school was the next day.

What a crazy time the middle 1960s were. It was hard enough being a pubescent teenager with all the confusion in our minds and changing bodies, but, the world around us was in utter chaos as well. Every time we turned on the TV, the programs took us to another dimension of fantasy. Then, in between programs, or in the news, we saw the awful images of the Vietnam War. We watched as the images would go from the colorful Monkees or Star Trek to the ravages of war with its dead bodies. It was painful for me to watch. Stories of sons, cousins, brothers, and friends always loomed. It made me feel scared and insecure. The only thing that was comforting was the music of the day and my girl-friends.

I recalled a lesson Sister had just taught us in school. The Vietnam War started in 1955. It was known as the Second Indochina War or American War and was fought in Asia. The fight was between North Vietnam and South Vietnam. North Vietnam was supported by the Communist countries. They were China, North Korea and the Soviet Union. South Vietnam was supported by the Capitalist countries Thailand, The Philippines, New Zealand, Australia, and the United States. The United States wanted to prevent a communist takeover of South Vietnam. They sent the first wave of troops — 3,500 Marines — in September 1965.

Despite Sister's lessons, I didn't really understand

why we were in Vietnam. What I did know was that I was against the war, any kind of war. I prayed for my cousin, Jim, from Ohio, for his safe return. There were so many protests and sit-ins.

My father always made comments about the war when the news came on. He did not support the war, but being a WWII veteran he believed that if a man was called to go to war he should go and fight. He became angry when he saw the kids burning the American flag and would say, "Don't these kids realize how many men lost their lives throughout the years for our freedom? Our flag represents that! Burning the flag or standing on it is morally wrong and reprehensible behavior! To make matters worse, these same protestors dishonor our poor Vets by spitting on them when they come back to the States! What's our nation coming to?"

Of course, we did not know the outcome of the war at that point in time. The monetary cost and casualties of approximately 58,220 men eventually led to the United States withdrawal by 1973. The Vietnamese lost over 3 million military and civilians combined on both sides. The war ended in 1975; South Vietnam fell to North Vietnam and then became a Communist Country.

I wanted to tune out these current event lessons and what Sister was teaching us about the war. I could not handle any more news about its violence. I just wanted it to all stop. I was a sensitive child and remembered everything, especially how hearing about it and seeing its images made me feel.

I had several conversations with my girlfriends about

the war, especially when the college kids started to burn their bras and draft cards in New York's Central Park. Glenda, Sara, and Patty did not seem to focus their attention on current events. Natalia had a sharp mind and was very interested in talking about everything. I liked that about her even if we butted heads on the subject, just like everything else. On the one hand, we agreed that we did not think the U.S. should be in Vietnam. However, it annoyed me that her view of America was usually slanted to the negative. At one point, out of curiosity, I asked her why she and her family lived here in the United States if they didn't like it. Why not just go back to South America if they thought it was so much better? Yikes, that did not go over well!

These turbulent times brought me back a few years earlier to 1962. The Cuban Missile Crisis took place from October 16–28, 1962. The confrontation was between the United States and the Soviet Union. The United States had a Ballistic Missile deployment in Turkey and Italy. The Soviet Union also had a Ballistic Missile deployment in Cuba. Everybody understood, including me, that the United States and the Soviet Union were pointing nuclear war heads at each other! The tense negotiation between President John F. Kennedy and Khrushchev ended when both sides agreed to dismantle the war heads. The United States also had to agree not to invade Cuba. This confrontation was considered the closest we had come to a nuclear war.

I remember how scared and vulnerable I felt at school when we practiced hiding under our desks with our hands on top of our heads. I almost wet my pants with fright. I couldn't tell if the drills were real or not. Would that bright light come and blow us all away?

One day I asked my father, "Pop, how come we're not building a shelter in our basement? Some of our neighbors are."

"Because, it would be better for us to die quickly instead of dragging it out!" he replied.

What a comforting thing to say to a nine-year-old. My mother chimed in and added, "You are too young to think about such things! Stop making a big deal out of everything!"

I think that's when I decided not to ask my parents too many questions or share my thoughts or feelings after that. What was the point? Never having a voice or being validated hurt too much. It was safer to keep quiet and to myself.

I remembered seeing the Watts riots on TV in 1965, a year after we arrived in Los Angeles. I had never seen such violence before and was horrified. It was still fresh in my mind and haunted my dreams.

When I learned about the Freedom Riders from reading one of my father's old newspaper articles I started to understand what prejudice and racism was all about. In my opinion, it was terrible to make Black people sit at the back of the bus. I thought the Freedom Riders were very brave and right to challenge the racial segregation when they rode the buses and tried to sit in the front. Good for them! This had all taken place years earlier in 1961, so I daydreamed about going back in time a few years so I could be there to sit alongside with them.

I watched Martin Luther King, the head of The Civil Rights Movement, give his speech "I Have a Dream," and was fascinated by it. He used his powerful speeches and non-violent resistance to make his point that, "All men are created equal!"

I did not know any Black people personally at the time, but wanted to. I thought it was terrible for people to hate someone just because the color of their skin was different. Besides, Sydney Poitier stole my heart in the movie, "To Sir with Love."

Little did I know that in the midst of the turbulent sixties my heart would start its own escapades with love.

"What the hell happened to your hair?" laughed.

I had covered my head with a scarf and did not make eye contact. I hurried to my desk and hid under the wooden lid. Everyone stared!

"What are you doing, Missy? Come out from under there! Take that off your head! It is not part of the uniform!" Sister snarled.

I reluctantly took it off and revealed the disaster that was once my long and brown, curly hair. It was now the color and consistency of straw. I had coveted Jenny's long and straight blonde, shiny hair that went down to her waist. Jack was a boy I had a crush on, but he had his eye on her.

I tried to create that Rapunzel hair for myself by using lemon and peroxide to make it blonde and this stuff called "Curl Free" to make it straight. Jenny was not as smart as the other "Goodie Two Shoes" girls and

e. It was not clear if she acted
father was a famous radio host or
in, absolutely beautiful, and seemed

s still rubbing his arm where I had
for saying I looked like a scarecrow when
ed, "Did you do this to change your
ce?"

th downcast eyes I nodded my head yes.

Vanity!!!" she bellowed. It is one of the seven
adly sins! You would do well to be grateful for what
God has already given you!"

I exhaled a deep breath. For the first time, what she said resonated with me.

That evening, my parents took me to get my hair cut and styled by a sweet lady named Barbara. She was a new friend of my parents and part of a huge, Italian family who eventually adopted us like family. Barbara performed a true miracle and styled my hair like Twiggy, the famous model. The groovy thing to do was to look like her. I knew the closest I could get was the haircut. There was no way I could ever get her stylish and skinny "Twiggy Figure." I was Italian after all — a little chubby and liked to eat. It was way too much pressure!

When I arrived at school the next day I rushed to Patty's desk while Sara stalled her from coming in the classroom. It was Patty's birthday. Glenda, Natalia and I waited for them to come into the classroom and for Patty to sit down. When she opened her desk and saw what was there, she smiled and laughed. I had pasted a huge picture of Davy Jones on the inside of her desk so she could see him every day. She was not allowed to put up any posters at home. I fantasized about putting Davy in a huge birthday cake to surprise her, but I knew that would never happen unless we were able to find him first. Daydreaming was becoming a regular habit of mine. I found myself fantasizing more and more like Danny Kaye did in "The Secret Life of Walter Mitty."

The Lavatory was right across the hall from our classroom. Most of the time, Sister would monitor and stand outside while we were in there. We were not allowed to talk. One day during recess, she was nowhere in sight. All five of us girls went in there, grabbed paper towels, wet them and threw them up onto the ceiling. Some of them kept falling down, but we kept it up until they stuck. Once again, we found ourselves hysterical with laughter. Haili happened to be in the bathroom as well so she joined in. She was very sweet and kind to everyone. She was the only one from "The Goodie Two Shoes" group who reached out and mingled with the rest of the class. She was absent from school quite often and never participated in any sports activities at recess. We thought it was because she was very overweight. We would learn later there was another reason as well.

Back in our seats, Sara lost her nerve and anxiously announced, "We better go back and take them down! Hurry, I'll stand guard!"

Sara peeked out into the hallway, looked both ways, and waved her hand to give the all clear.

Glenda grabbed the 12-foot stick that opened and closed the windows while Natalia held the other end.

They ran across the hall to the bathroom to remove the towels from the ceiling with the stick. Patty and I followed. We quickly threw the towels into the garbage bin, mopped up the water that was all over the floor and ran back into the classroom just before the bell rang.

Sister entered the room and sat at her desk and opened the lesson book. She was about to speak when the long stick Glenda used fell down on the floor with the loudest clang! You could have heard a pin drop! Unlike the boys, who actually went through with their pranks, we girls usually chickened out. As our eyes met, I noticed the slightest smirks on their faces. That's when I knew that they were as glad as I was that we made the attempt.

Sister looked around with narrow eyes and studied our faces. I prayed that she would not notice how out of breath we were. Her eyes landed on Paul and the usual suspects, but then as usual, rested on Casey. I swear, I was just waiting for her to target him again so this time I could save him and confess. I guess there did not seem to be a clear offense, so she proceeded with the lesson.

These rebellious, childish pranks could have gotten us a beating, but it was worth it. One day, we threw Natalia in the same closet that Casey frequented. I don't remember why. It was probably because she always had a highfalutin air about her that annoyed the crap out of us.

Chapter Fourteen

FROM CRAYONS TO PERFUME

Every Easter, Disneyland hosted Catholic School Day. Our class got to go. What a treat! Once we were there, Sister corralled all of us in The Tiki Tiki Room. Natalia's mom drove us and was our designated chaperone. We begged her to let us go off on our own. Unbeknownst to Sister, we flew the coop. We had a blast on the rides and spent most of the day on Tom Sawyer's Island. I did not want to come down from the trees I had climbed. They reminded me of the trees in Cleveland that I climbed and played in when I was a child.

Jack, Robert, Preston, Paul, and Ronnie ran in packs, just like we did. When they found us, they convinced us to ride The Matterhorn with them. Looking over our shoulders, hoping that Sister wouldn't see us, we paired up and went for the ride.

Jack was a year-and-a-half older than the rest of us. He was big and strong. His dirty blond hair and green eyes were hard to resist. He was a bad boy and the leader of the pack. I was naturally drawn to him and very happy when he asked me to be his girlfriend. He sat behind me on the Matterhorn and kept copping a feel of my breast the entire time in spite of my sharp elbow blows to his stomach. I did not speak to him for the rest of the trip for taking advantage of me like that. He kept laughing at me and enlisted the rest of the goofballs to laugh as well. It was not funny!

At the end of the day at twilight, the girls and I stood in the center of Market Street. We watched Tinkerbell fly across the sky to light the fireworks as the Disney songs played in the background. It transported our minds back to the Magic Kingdom and fairy tales — the place I wanted to remain forever and never grow up.

For the next few days, Jack apologized several times, but I did not forgive him until he invited me over to his house for dinner. He lived in the Canyon, five minutes from Glenda. After dinner, I was going to go over to her house to spend the night. I was thrilled to meet his family. They were from Hungary. I can still taste his mom's delicious Hungarian Goulash.

Jack had an appetite, but it was not for his mom's cooking! He told his parents we were going to go upstairs to the bonus room to play games and pool. His bedroom was off to the side. We slipped inside his bedroom. I noticed a silver necklace with a heart-shaped pendant. Hoping he intended it for me, I held the necklace up and asked, "Whose necklace is this?"

He avoided the question and announced, "We are going to Preston's house in an hour."

"I can't go to Preston's because Glenda and the girls are waiting for me."

"They can wait," he bellowed.

He practically threw me on his bed, hungrily inhaled me while he kept grinding me down onto the bed. I was going to protest at first, but was quickly consumed with passion. This was the first time I had ever engaged in hot and heavy necking. Time stood still, all reason went right out the window. Then, his little brother appeared in the doorway.

We both got up quickly and went back into the bonus room. We were fully clothed and soaked in perspiration. I didn't know if it was mine or his. My head was swirling with a myriad of thoughts. I quickly came to my senses and was thankful I got out of there with my virginity still intact. Now I discovered what that song, "I Think We're Alone Now," was all about. I realized I should have never put myself in that position and promised myself not to do it again. I was amazed at how hard it was to control these new found urges. What was left of my reputation was completely shot! And, oh my gosh, how in the world was I going to confess this at church?

We left his house and started to walk down the street toward Glenda's house. He stopped at a pick-up truck that was parked on the side of the road. He opened the door of the truck and fiddled under the dashboard. When the truck started he said, "Get in."

"But I…"

"We have to stop by Preston's house first to pick him up, then I'll drop you off," he interrupted.

I lost track of time as we drove around stopping at a few of his friends' houses. They all seemed much older than we were. He was picking something up and dropping it off elsewhere. I was having such a great time feeling the warm night air in my hair and thinking this was like being on a real date, until we reached the last stop. It was Jenny's house, the girl with the golden, Rapunzel hair.

Jack got out of the car and talked with her for about ten minutes while I waited in the car with Preston. He could see I was angry and honked the horn for Jack to return.

"What the hell is going on?" I blurted out.

Not meeting my eyes, Preston responded, "Hey, I'm just along for the ride, like you. If you want to know what's going on, you'll have to ask him."

"Ask him what?"

"Oh, I don't know, maybe how come he is driving when he is only 15-years-old? Whose truck is this? Who were those guys and what is he doing with Jenny? Just sayin!"

Boy, did I feel like a dummy. I was so wrapped up in my adolescent fantasy that I could not see what was really happening. After all, I was just a kid and as they say, I couldn't see the forest for the trees. All I wanted to do at that point was get to Glenda's.

Not a word was spoken as Jack drove me to Glenda's house. The only sound was the radio ironically playing, "How Can I Be Sure," from The Young Rascals. Pinching back my tears, I realized that the words in the song were exactly how I was feeling.

We finally got to Glenda's house at 2:15 a.m. I snuck in through the back stairs to Glenda's room. They were all still awake, except for Patty. She always fell asleep first.

"Diane! Where were you?" Glenda snapped.

"We were frantic and had no way of getting in touch with you!"

"Does your mom know?" I asked.

"No! Thank God, we covered for you!"

I told them everything that happened. Glenda warned me that I could have gotten arrested or something. We still were not sure what he was up to with his friends. Sara was shocked at my escapade in Jack's room. Natalia's pouty lips were now pursed and her eyes narrowed a bit. She was unusually quiet.

As I lay there trying to fall asleep that same song kept playing over in my mind, which questioned how I could be sure. This was the second time I thought I was in love.

Of course it was just a crush, but young emotions are all consuming and confusing. All the love songs from the '50s and '60s were ever present in my mind. "At Last," "The Look of Love," "Unchained Melody," "When a Man Loves a Women," "My Brown Eyed Girl," "In My Life," "I'm a Believer," and countless others spoke to me. These songs influenced my concept of what love was supposed to be. I knew every word and still do. I was certain somewhere, somehow, all these songs would become true for me when my Knight in Shining Armor on a steed appeared. If all these people sang about this thing called "Love," it must true, right?

Everything started to change when Sgt. Pepper's Lonely Hearts Club Band was released. It was the soundtrack of The Summer of Love. We started to see everything from a different perspective. We slowly went from our conservative, religious views to worldly ones. The album cover alone was a colorful work of art with the lyrics printed on the inside. We tried to solve the mystery and discover if Paul was really dead. The music sounded like a concert. It introduced our young minds to Eastern spirituality and ideologies. The concept of drugs literally transcended us to another dimension. We were too young to consider the drugs, but it left the door open in our minds to the possibility someday. Our world was opening up as we sang and celebrated our new theme song, "With A Little Help From My Friends." Even though we loved and listened to the music of the other bands, The Monkees were still our favorite. Their childlike personas on the TV show were more relatable to us.

The next morning, Glenda and I slept in while the rest of the girls went home early. We had plans to go to the movies later in the day. Glenda's mom drove us to The Cinerama Dome on Sunset Boulevard to see the movie "Camelot." I had just enough money for the movie ticket from what I earned babysitting. In those days, $1.25 was a lot of money.

I was captivated by this story about King Arthur and The Knights of the Round Table. His vision and quest was to create a civilized world amongst the Medieval barbaric existence that they lived in at the time.

"Might for Right!" "Right for Right!" "Justice for

All!" Camelot was the heart of everything that was good in them. It was something to fight and even die for to keep it alive. The hopeless love triangle between King Arthur, Guinevere, and Sir Lancelot was something I would later relate to. They all loved each other, but the heartbreaking betrayal would ultimately destroy them all.

Yet, Arthur's ability to forgive Guinevere was astounding. He put his love for his Jennie/Guinevere and Lancelot above his own pride and pain. And somehow, it all resonated with me. I had no judgment for them, just a new found understanding of what it meant to be human. Glenda and I became hysterical, and could not get up to leave our seats for at least 45 minutes after the movie ended. It changed my perspective of life.

Movies that captured and molded this young American girl's heart created a hopeless and or hopeful perennial romantic. Movies such as "Camelot," "West Side Story," and "Splendor in the Grass" with Natalie Wood and Warren Beatty, as well as songs including, "If Ever I Would Leave You" and "There's a Place For Us," absolutely destroyed me. I still cry when I think of them. "The Graduate" was an eye-opener because I never thought people over 40 had sex. How could she? How could he? These were the questions a young girl could not ask, understand, or even want to know the answer to!

Chapter Fifteen

EDELWEISS

The school put on a play each year. This year, it was an Operetta called "In Grand Old Switzerland," written by Otis M. Carrington in the 1930s. In a small village in Switzerland, two star-crossed kids become infatuated with each other while their fathers' hate for one another grows. It is similar to the Romeo and Juliet story.

To my surprise, I got the lead role of Trudi. I was going to sing a solo and a couple of duets and had a lot of lines to remember and act out. Casey played my father. He was so talented and played the grumpy, overprotective father with perfection. Patti had a huge roll and played Mrs. Miller, an American tourist. Natalia played Hedwig, Trudi's friend. Glenda and Sara were in the chorus. Juli, Trudi's love interest, was played by a seventh grader named Michael, who was darling. Our group spent several weeks rehearsing.

When the big night came, everyone was nervous and

excited. Back stage, I suddenly became overwhelmed with self-doubt and stage fright. Casey saw me pacing back and forth and wringing my hands. He stopped and asked, "What's the matter?"

"What if I forget my lines? I practically faint when I have to go up to the board in class! What made me think I could do this? Agh, I am so stupid!" I was now bent over not able to breathe.

"Stop saying that!" Casey demanded. "You have been just fine in rehearsals and tonight is no different. You can do this!" he encouraged.

Then he leaned over, patted me on my back and whispered in my ear, "Now breathe through your nose slowly and try to relax."

After a moment he asked, "Better?"

"Yes," I replied.

"Okay good. I have to hurry and get dressed."

I was still lingering at the end of the hallway, trying to hide from everyone else, when Michael appeared.

"Oh, there you are. Can I rehearse my love song with you one more time?" he asked.

"Okay," I agreed.

There was a scene where Juli sings a love song to Trudi. After the song, they were supposed to embrace. Obviously, we were not allowed to do that. On stage we almost kiss when Trudi's father calls out and interrupts them.

But at that moment when we rehearsed the scene, we went in for the kiss and not only did it, but kissed again. No one saw us. I think that might have been Michael's first kiss. I must have needed some more comforting and that kiss definitely helped. I felt a little guilty because I cheated on Jack. But did I really? I thought we had an unspoken agreement between us. But he was not paying much attention to me and I was not sure where I stood with him. I could not bring myself to confront him about Jenny.

Just before the play began, I peeked out into the audience. My big sister, Cindy, was in the audience. She actually came to see me perform and brought Billy Mumy from the television show "Lost in Space" with her! I was ecstatic that she was there! The play was a success for everyone. I was so happy I pushed myself to work through my fears and felt more confident after that.

After the play, Jack came back stage to congratulate me. When he saw Michael standing next to me, he practically pushed him out of the way and gave me a big kiss. Now I knew I was a bad girl for kissing two boys on the same day! It wasn't that I didn't like kissing two boys, but I never wanted to hurt Michael. Jack, on the other hand, was someone who would hurt me.

Chapter Sixteen

THE CONFESSIONAL

Every Wednesday morning the student body went to chapel and confession. This was a ritual I never enjoyed. The confessional was this tiny, dark double stall separated by a thin wooden panel. The window was a screen you could see through between the Priest and the person confessing.

Everyone kept tabs on how many Rosaries and Hail Mary's Father Francis would dish out for penance. The more the girls received meant they were considered "bad." The boys had a different scenario. The more penance they had to do, the cooler they were considered. They would actually high five and pat each other on the back!

Patty and I were standing in line to go into the confessional. She was in front of me. I leaned in and whispered in her ear, "P…"

"What?" she whispered back without turning her head.

"I hate going in there. It's such a small space it makes me feel claustrophobic and then I can't breathe!"

"SHUSH," she replied.

"Why is that screen even there if you can see right through it? Father Francis can always tell who you are!" I protested.

"SHUSH!" she repeated.

"But, once you go in, there is nowhere to hide and you have to tell the truth!" I insisted.

"For Pete's sake Diane, do you want to get us in trouble? Zip it!"

"Well, I guess there is only one good thing about it…" I continued.

"If I ask you what, will you shut up?" she snapped.

"The good thing is that after you confess and say your penance, your soul is clean. You get to start all over again," I giggled.

Rolling her eyes and shaking her head, she entered the confessional. I don't know what in the world she confessed, but you could have heard Father Francis yelling at her from a mile away. She emerged from the confessional slamming the door as she exited. Her skin was beet red, her lips pursed, and her eyes were downcast. She ran out of the church before I could ask her what happened.

Crap! I was next! I was going to confess what happened with Jack in his room, but when I got in there, I hyperventilated again and thought I was going to faint. I thought better of it and said, "Bless me Father for I have sinned. It's been two weeks since my last confession. I took the name of the Lord in vain twice, I kissed two boys on the same day, and I lied to my parents. I said it fast hoping he would not really hear me.

"WHAT!" he bellowed. "Who were the boys?"

When I did not tell him he yelled even louder. Finally, he dismissed me and gave me two Rosaries and five extra Hail Mary's for penance. I wanted the earth to swallow me up. Considering where I was, I had no choice but to come out of the confessional to face the nuns' judging eyes, the entire student body, and the boys' snickering laughs.

When Jack went in, everyone seemed to watch the confessional instead of praying. We heard yelling again. It did not surprise me, knowing some of the shenanigans he was into. In the confessional Jack said, "Bless me Father for I have sinned. It's been three weeks since my last confession. I did some things with girls."

"What things?" Father Francis asked.

"I'm sorry Father, but I cannot say," Jack replied.

"Was it Diane?" Father demanded.

"I'm sorry Father, but I cannot say," Jack repeated.

"Was it Glenda? Natalia? Jenny?" Father Francis insisted.

"I'm sorry Father, but I cannot say," Jack stubbornly repeated.

More yelling.

Jack came out of the confessional smiling. All the boys were waiting with bated breath. I tried to hide under the seat. Peter, Robert, Preston, Ronnie, and Paul leaned into the pew towards Jack.

"What did you get?" Peter whispered.

"Five Rosaries and three good leads!" Jack announced.

High fives ensued all around.

I snuck out of the church before our class was dismissed from Chapel. I found Patty in the lavatory stall. She didn't want to come out. Through the door I asked, "What happened? Are you all right?"

No answer.

"Come on P, come out of there."

Without a word she came out and walked outside. I followed behind and said, "Okay, no one is around, what did you confess? Father Francis screamed the loudest at you!"

Patty was the angriest I had ever seen her and replied, "All I told him was that when I go for walks I sometimes pray directly to Jesus to confess my sins."

"So what's wrong with that? I do that too sometimes, but go to confession as well. What did Father Francis say about it?" I asked.

"Father screamed at me and said, 'How dare you! That is the sin of presumption! You can only be forgiven through confession and absolution! You have to come to me for that!'"

Shaking her fist toward the church, Patty then declared, "I'm done! I'm never going to Confession again!"

As our class exited the church, we slipped back in line with them and walked back into the school building. Casey was right behind us. In the hallway, a little girl named Jilly, who Patty babysat, was standing against the door of her classroom. She was a chubby, redheaded little girl and there was no mistaking why her eyes were full of tears. There was a wad of gum on the end of her nose. She just looked up at us, but did not say a word.

Casey, Patti, and I stopped short. Just as I pulled the gum off her nose Sister appeared.

"What are you doing? Get back to class this instant!" she snarled.

"My God, can't you find a kinder way to talk to us?" I protested.

As the rest of the class looked on, I stepped in front of Jilly and held the gum up in Sister's face. She raised her hand to smack me when Casey and Patti both stepped in front of me and grabbed her hand to stop the blow.

Chapter Seventeen

REVELATION

Not a word was spoken. Casey stared her down while Patty pushed Sister's hand away. Patty was so angry I thought she was going to kill her right then and there. Sister stepped back in stunned silence. Then she told Jilly to go back into her classroom. To our amazement, without saying a word, Sister quietly walked in front of us and back to the classroom. She went straight to her desk and sat down. We all followed and did the same.

We finally stood up to her. She knew it, we knew it, and that was the end of it. Sister stopped bullying all of us after that day. She actually started to encourage us in a positive way. The other boys backed off as well and finally stopped doing their stupid pranks. I started to believe in miracles. It was an imperative reckoning that opened an enlightened pathway to change and growth for all of us, including Sister. And with reckoning came future revelations.

In light of all that had happened, there were a couple of changes and paths Patty and I made that may have not been the best. Patty quit the choir and just like me, our parents didn't know about it because they never went to Mass. Our school was near Fairfax and Sunset Boulevard. Instead of going to Mass on Sunday morning, we would meet in the schoolyard and then walk to the Thrifty Drug on Sunset Boulevard right across the street from the Sunfax Market. This became one of our new after school hangouts with the rest of the girls. We enjoyed sitting at the soda fountain counter while we drank sodas and ate their delicious ice cream. The old juke box still worked and provided hours of music and entertainment.

The following Sunday, my brother, Gino, made his Confirmation. The sacrament of Confirmation is a Catholic sacrament. It is believed that the recipient is sealed with the gift of The Holy Spirit, and that their Christian faith is strengthened.

My mother was an amazing cook and made an incredible feast for our family. She also invited my brother's confirmation sponsor as well. His name was Richard. He was also a producer who was helping Cindy with her movie career. His wife, Suzanna, was beautiful inside and out. I was drawn to her. Of all my mom's friends in California, I liked her the most because she actually conversed with me. When she spoke, her voice was resolute and confident and her diction emphatic.

Richard ate course after course of my mother's cuisine with a passion. He was small in stature so I wondered where he put it all. Richard and Susanna gave Gino a beautiful Bible as a gift. That was the first time I had ever seen a Bible up close. The only other Bible I saw was displayed on the Altar at church. Before we ate our meal, we said the usual blessing: "Bless us, Oh Lord and these thy gifts…"

I noticed that Suzanna said the words, but did not make the sign of the cross. I leaned towards her and quietly asked, "Why didn't you make the sign of the cross?"

"I say the prayer, but don't make the sign of the cross because I pray differently. I am a Protestant, a Born Again Christian," she revealed.

I was intrigued and asked, "What is a Protestant and what is Born Again?"

She was about to tell me, but we were interrupted by Mother's delicious cream puffs placed before us. Later that evening, I told Suzanna what happened to Patty and asked, "Do you believe we can confess our sins directly to God?"

"Absolutely!" she replied and went on to say, "The Bible says in First Timothy 2:5, 'For there is one God and one mediator between God and men, the man Christ Jesus.' In Philippians 4:6-7 it says, 'Do not be anxious about anything, but in everything, by prayer and petition, with thanksgiving, present your request to God and the peace of God, which transcends all understanding, will guard your hearts and your minds in Christ Jesus.'"

"So, does that mean it is okay to confess our sins and ask God for what we need directly?"

"Exactly!" Suzanna emphatically agreed. "Confession is vital to our salvation. Write down this Bible verse and look it up. Romans 10:9-10, 'Because if you confess with your mouth that Jesus is Lord and believe in your heart that God raised him from the dead, you will be saved. For with the heart one believes and is justified, and with the mouth one confesses and is saved.'"

She then explained, "To be Born Again, you need to confess your sins and ask Jesus to come into your heart. Ask Him to be your Lord and Savior and trust in His finished work on the Cross. You can't earn your way into Heaven, no one can. Jesus earned your way to heaven by dying on the cross for you. He paid the price for all of your sins."

She then offered me one more verse. "Ephesians 2:8-9, 'For it is by grace you have been saved, through faith, and this not from yourselves, it is a gift of God – not by works, so that no one can boast.'"

I wrote down the Bible verses and looked them up later that night when I went to bed. I was practically hiding under the sheets, I was so afraid. We were told in school that only the priest could read the Bible and interpret it for us. If we even considered any other religious teachings other than our Catholic catechism, it was considered a mortal sin and we would go to hell. I kept those Bible verses somewhere in the back of my mind anyway and continued to pray and confess to Jesus directly.

Suzanna shared many Bible verses and pearls of wisdom whenever I saw her. I learned and remembered the following from her:

- *"Don't take God's sacrifice on the Cross and His free gift of salvation through Jesus Christ for granted. It's not a get out of jail free card you can take it in and out of your pocket whenever it suits you."*
- *"You must walk the walk if you claim to be a Christian."*
- *"You will recognize a true believer of God by his fruits and that goes for you as well."*
- *"Don't judge others lest you be judged."*
- *"Be kind and loving to all."*
- *"Always remember, that the status of a penitent is more important that a self-righteous person."*

These character building truths, based on Bible verses, were exactly what I needed to hear. I did not realize it then, but the seeds of the Gospel were being planted and the harvest of my salvation was just a matter of time.

Now that I knew I could confess directly to God, I did not go to confession as much. I would still go into the church when no one was there and pray to Saint Theresa, my patron Saint from Confirmation and The Virgin Mary. I would stare at the Tabernacle on the Altar and fantasize about opening those tiny, golden doors to see if God was really in there.

On Good Friday, the Stations of the Cross was a ritual prayer and practice I would never miss. It made me connect with Christ on His journey. I understood that He sacrificed Himself and died for me so I could go to Heaven. I never wanted to forget that.

My secret desire was to be picked for the May

Crowning. I went to so many of them in grade school. If you got picked, I thought it meant that you were favored by God. After all, you were Crowning His Mother with beautiful rose flower crowns, right? It was like being the Virgin Mary herself.

I knew I would probably not be picked because my grades were bad, I was a bit rebellious, I goofed off in class, and flirted with the boys. But still, I prayed and hoped. If I got picked maybe then I would be special and my parents would see me for once in my invisible existence at home.

But alas! No cigar! I was not picked. But, one of the "Goodie Two Shoes" was picked, Peggy. Only an eighth grade girl can crown the Virgin Mary. It was a huge ceremony. That was my only chance. There would be no more May Crownings after this. So, through my tears, I sang "Ave" "Ave" "Ave" Regina!" with the rest of the class.

Patty stood next to me. She knew why I was crying and said, "For Pete's sake Diane, it's not the end of the world. Get over it! Besides, I need you to take over a babysitting job for me later today. Can you do it?"

"Okay sure, which one is it?"

"You have been there with me before. It's for little Jilly and Sarah."

I wasn't looking forward to being in their home, but I accepted nonetheless.

Chapter Eighteen

THE BROWN SHOES

Sometimes, I would go with Patty to her babysitting jobs. She lived two miles from my house. I got around quite well on my skateboard. A year earlier, on one of her babysitting jobs, we watched a brand new show called "Star Trek." It was the very first episode that featured a Greek God named "Apollo." I could not decide who was more handsome, Apollo or Captain Kirk. That was my introduction to Greek Mythology and a place called space, "Where no man had gone before!" I became a Trekkie and a sci-fi lover that day.

At first, I was thrilled to get this babysitting job, but then I learned more about the family…things that made me uneasy. Still, the little girls were adorable. Jilly was the girl with the gum on her nose at school. Her little sister, Sarah, was a tiny version of her, but very talkative. Their mom would go out every Saturday at noon and stay out until just before dusk. She reeked of alcohol and swaggered in when she returned. It disgusted me. I worried about those kids and tried to be as loving as I could with them. I wondered what their mom was doing when she was gone and how she really treated them. The house was dirty and they seemed neglected. I did not want to go back every Saturday, but I did so for the girls. They needed me.

But in spite of wanting to help them, something happened one evening at dusk that changed everything and I never went back.

On my way home, as I walked as fast as I could before it became really dark, I sensed someone following me. I crossed the street and glanced back and thought I saw a man. Okay, maybe he was not following me because he seemed to be at least a few apartment buildings down. I crossed the street again. Sweet Mother of God, he crossed too! It was too dark at this point to see him clearly, but I knew, I absolutely knew, he was behind me. I could not breathe, I walked faster! My throat tightened and I could not call out! I walked quickly into an apartment complex on my left. I turned right and walked up the stairs.

There were two doors at the top of the stairs. I opened the screen door on my right and knocked on the door. I pretended the door opened and began to speak to the person who lived there. I mimicked a man's voice in a desperate attempt to fake the stalker out.

I looked down the dark stairwell and saw only the tips of his brown shoes at the bottom! He was standing right behind the wall! I knew he was there. The light shown only on the tips of his brown, pointy shoes.

I did not remember anything after that and never

knew what happened. I had a sense of his shoes turning and hearing footsteps leave. The next morning I sat up in bed with an anxious start. I think that was my first panic attack. I experienced traumatic dreams where I felt lost and anxiously tried to find my way back home. I never told anyone about that awful night until years later.

Chapter Nineteen

WHEN THINGS GO WRONG

The last few months of the school year were busy. I struggled to keep up with the assignments. On Monday morning Sister announced, "I have some good news. The acceptance letters from the high schools you applied for have arrived."

As she passed them out, I started to feel light-headed again. We had made our submissions and took tests at three different Catholic High Schools. They were painfully difficult for me. I really did not think I would be accepted anywhere. It actually did not matter to me which school I would go to as long as all of us girls were going to stay together.

The smartest and richest girls got accepted to Marymount; Sara was one of them. Glenda and Patty got accepted to Providence High School. Natalia and I got accepted to Notre Dame High School. Our grade point average had to be higher to get into Providence. This upset me terribly because we would have to travel at least fifteen miles to and from our home and take three different buses. It upset me mostly because we were all going to be split apart. We made a promise that we would stay in touch with each other forever, no matter what.

Now that graduation was only six weeks away Sister Mary Margret, our Principal, explained everything we needed to accomplish. We started practicing for our graduation day. There were many speeches, awards, and songs we had to learn. Surprised, but happy to hear, she announced that the school was actually going to give us a graduation party/hootenanny in the hall.

When we gathered together in the choir room to practice for graduation, something unexpected happened. We were lining up on the bleachers when all of sudden Haili fell from the very top bleacher onto the floor. We stared in shock as she shook all over with arms and legs jerking about.

"What in the world is happening to her?" I whispered to Natalia.

Not answering, she shrugged her shoulders and just stared at Haili.

I was so embarrassed for her because her underpants were showing in full view. I thought the boys would laugh, but they didn't.

None of us could move or speak. It was the first time we had ever witnessed an epileptic seizure. The collective empathy for our classmate was apparent on every single face as we watched the paramedics whisk her away to the hospital. She did not regain consciousness. We never knew until that day what poor Haili had to endure. Traumatic experiences seem to bond people together more than anything else. For the first time without being told, we prayed.

The next morning in class Sister hesitated a moment, then she announced, "This morning we need to pray for Haili because she is still in a coma."

Clearly shaken, Tara gasped, "What does that mean?"

"It means she is sleeping and can't wake up on her own," Ellie blurted out. This was the first time she did not raise her hand to speak.

"The doctors and prayer will help her wake up; so let's keep on praying!" Sister replied, with deep conviction.

Ellie, Peggy, and Tara all sat next to each other in class. They held hands and prayed quietly while they looked at Haili's empty seat. We all bowed our heads to join in.

When they finished their prayer, Sister spoke again, "I'm so sorry to give you more upsetting news, but we need pray for Glenda as well."

"What?!" I gasped.

"Why, what happened?!" Patty demanded.

"All I can tell you is that she was rushed to the hospital last night for exploratory surgery. Alright class, let's bow our heads again.

My heart sank as the entire class just looked at each other with tears in their eyes. Frank and Preston's heads went down into their folded arms on the top of their desks. All of this was just too much for any of us to take. We did not have access to phones so we sat in agony all day not knowing what had happened to Glenda or Haili's fate.

FINALLY AFTER SCHOOL, PATTY AND I WALKED TO HER house. Her mom was an ICU nurse at the same hospital where both Haili and Glenda were located.

"Glenda had several tumors and one of them was the size of a grapefruit on her ovary. Don't worry though, it is not cancer and they got it all out," she said quickly as she scurried about.

I breathed out a sigh of relief and said, "Oh, thank God! Maybe that's why she could never get rid of her big belly no matter how much she tried to diet."

Then, she added, "Unfortunately, they also had to take out one of her ovaries."

"Does that mean she will not be able to have children?" Patty asked.

"No one knows for sure because she still has one ovary."

"And what about Haili?" I asked.

An awkward silence ensued as Patty's mom simply shook her head. "We don't know yet."

We had to simply wait.

I spent the night at Patty's house. It was the one and only time she was allowed to have a sleepover. We spent the evening constructing a comic book starring, "The Peanuts Gang and The Grapefruit." Patty and I wrote it and I did all the drawings. We had to get it done by the next day because we planned to give it to Glenda in the hospital.

We were so consumed with writing the book that I did not notice how quiet the house was until later. Her parents and brother were all home, but there was no conversation, television sounds, just silence. I realized later what Patty had told us at the pajama party was true. No one was allowed to come out of their rooms. I could not wait to get the hell out of there. I realized how much I appreciated my crazy, noisy Italian family!

The next morning was no different from my house on a Saturday morning. Endless chores! I helped her with them and then we had to go to my house so I could finish mine. My sister offered to drive us to the hospital to see Glenda so we needed to be ready by 12 noon. As Patty's mom was leaving the house for the hospital, she told Patty she did not want her to go to the hospital and did not say why. Her dad said she could go anyway and made us breakfast. They had several ducks so he fried up the best eggs I ever tasted! I fell in love with one of the baby ducklings so he packed the duckling up for me to keep and drove us to my house.

We finished all of my chores quickly and hid the duckling in the bathtub. Just as we were about to leave I heard my Nonny, who was visiting from Cleveland scream, "Ooooh Ma Ma!"

Yep! She had discovered the duckling in the bathtub. It had crapped all over the place! Cindy, Patty, and I were hysterical trying to clean the tub while my mom tried to keep my Nonny from fainting. It was the first time in a long time that Cindy and I actually had fun together. I could tell she enjoyed it as well. She nicknamed Patty "QUACK QUACK" and called her that from then on. After we finished cleaning up, we rushed back to Patty's, returned the duckling and drove to Natalia's to collect her and Sara.

When we arrived at Natalia's house, she and Sara and her mom were already in the car pulling out of the driveway. They all seemed very upset. Waving her hands for us to follow, Natalia yelled, "Hurry up! Glenda is in critical condition. The surgery was harder than expected on her."

Making the situation even more dire was the fact that Haili still hadn't woken up. We followed in silence to St. John's Hospital. Both girls were in the ICU just a few doors from each other. The waiting room and hallway of the ICU was packed with familiar faces of family and friends of both girls. Everyone seemed very upset and some were crying.

Patty's mom was the attending nurse and glared at her for showing up. She was too busy to confront Patty. She scurried back and forth telling everyone they could not be in there, but no one listened.

In the hallway, some of the girls from our class had arrived before us. They were surrounding Barbara Jean, who was sitting on her legs on the floor flailing her arms up and down and sobbing. At first I did not think much of it because she was highly emotional and given to tantrums. It was not the first time we had seen her collapse onto the ground and cry. I felt guilty because I had been avoiding her ever since I spent the night and got drunk at her house a few weeks before. Something else was really strange and different about her, but I could not put my finger on it.

As we approached, Natalia sarcastically said, "I wonder what drama story she's spinning now?"

We all stopped as Patty leaned over and asked Barbara Jean, "What's going on?"

"She's dead! She's dead!" she wailed.

"Who?" Sara gasped.

"Which one?" Patty yelled.

"I don't know for sure..." Barbara Jean admitted, "but she doesn't look right."

Time stood still. The room swayed in and out for a moment, I could not see and almost passed out. Patty held onto me as she dragged me down the hall. Haili's room was filled with people. We could barely see her. I had never seen anyone in that condition before. She was unconscious with breathing tubes and monitors everywhere. Was she unconscious or dead?

In spite of all the people in the room, no one spoke. Then we heard the beeping sound. It was the only sound on the floor. Haili's heart beat! We were relieved to hear it for a moment, but then another thought occurred to us. Where was the other beat? With eyes wide and trembling bodies, we looked at one another in disbelief. Our Glenda was gone! We seemed to be floating further down the hall in slow motion to her room. All the sound had disappeared except for the beating of my heart.

Glenda's family surrounded her bed. All we could see were her bare feet at first. And there she was, lying on her bed. There was no sound in the room. Her family was now staring at all of us. Then…Glenda's eyes opened!

"AUGGGG!!!"

A collective simultaneous cry of joy erupted as we sobbed and held each other up! Glenda was too weak to speak, but her parents assured us that she was going to be alright. Natalia started to say, "Glenda, when we didn't hear your heart monitor we thought…"

I jumped in and said, "We knew you were going to be okay, besides we have to find Davy Jones, right? So hurry up and get better!"

We had all been so busy with our school work and high school submissions that we had not had the time to go back to Wonderland.

"Davy Jones?" Cindy asked.

"Yes," I said and proceeded to tell her how long we had been looking for him.

"Really? Why didn't you tell me about it before?"

"I don't know, you have been so busy making your movie and I didn't think you would be interested."

"Well, I am!" she assured me. She smiled and patted me on the head as if she was planning something.

As we left Glenda's room, Natalia emphatically declared, "I'm going to kill her!"

"Who?" asked Sara.

"Barbara Jean!"

"No! No!" Patty replied.

"Let it go! She was just being dramatic as usual!"

I was still too shaken to say anything, but I knew that Patty was just as scared as the rest of us, but did not want to admit it. We almost lost our "Bunny" and were now all grateful and relieved that she was still with us.

A few days later, we found that for the first time, Barbara Jean's theatrics were not unmerited. Haili never woke up and we were forever changed.

Chapter Twenty

REQUIEM

Our class instinctively congregated in the back of the church. Patty, Natalia, Sara, and I stayed close to one another as we blessed ourselves with the holy water. Our class formed a single line as we slowly ascended toward the Altar. The church was packed and looked beautiful at night adorned by candles and flowers. Sister saved two rows for her class in the front of the church.

There it was. I froze. Patty nudged me forward. The closer we got to the casket, the tighter I twisted my rosary beads around my fingers. With our arms linked together, we approached the casket and stared down. None of us had ever seen a dead person before. I did not know what to expect and was surprised at how beautiful and peaceful Haili appeared. She looked like she was sleeping. But she wasn't sleeping or breathing; Haili was dead.

After we were seated, Monsignor Enzo closed the

casket and sprinkled holy water on it as Father Francis dispersed the burning incense toward it and the congregation. The incense smoke was oppressive and always made me feel nauseated. They both said the Mass and administered Holy Communion.

I could barely hear what Father Francis was saying. My mind kept asking Jesus, "Why did she have to die? She was so sweet, so young. Her entire life was ahead of her. Her story was not finished. What is the point of all this?"

Father Francis caught my attention when he quoted Ecclesiastes 3:1-8 Verses:

1. *To everything there is a season, and a time to every purpose under the heaven:*
2. *a time to be born, and a time to die; a time to plant, and a time to pluck up that which is planted;*
3. *a time to kill, and a time to heal; a time to break down, and a time to build up;*
4. *a time to weep, and a time to laugh; a time to mourn, and a time to dance;*
5. *a time to cast away stones, and a time to gather stones together; a time to embrace, and a time to refrain from embracing;*
6. *a time to seek and a time to lose; a time to keep, and a time to cast away;*
7. *a time to tear, and a time to sew; a time to keep silence, and a time to speak;*
8. *a time to love, and a time to hate; a time of war, and a time of peace.*

Where had I heard that before? Then I realized those were the words from the song "Turn Turn Turn" that the band The Byrds recorded. I never knew the lyrics for that song were taken from the Bible.

Father Francis went on to say that when someone we love dies, we may feel devastated and robbed. We can keep them alive in our hearts by continuing to love them and share our memories of them. He also referenced 1 Thessalonians 4:13-14 "Brothers and sisters, we do not want you to be uninformed about those who sleep in death, so that you do not grieve like the rest of mankind, who have no hope. For we believe that Jesus died and rose again, and so we believe that God will bring with Jesus those who have fallen asleep in Him." I understood and believed this Bible verse and it gave me comfort to know I would see Haili again in Heaven someday. Her body was here, but her spirit lives on in Heaven with Jesus.

WE HAD GIVEN GLENDA TIME TO RECOVER AT HOME, as did the rest of us in the aftermath of Haili's death. We had a lot on our minds, but hadn't spoken for a few days since the funeral. Patty finally broke our unspoken silence and need to grieve on our own terms by asking me to come with her to visit Glenda. After her mother led us into her room, we climbed into her big canopy bed beside her, held her hand and read our comic book to her. It was very funny and made her laugh. It felt good to laugh after all of the sadness we had recently endured. But, the fear still remained behind her eyes. She was brave and told us, "Don't worry about me you guys, I'll be…"

"Glenda, did you know about the tumors?" Patty interrupted.

"I knew something was wrong because my stomach was always so swollen."

"Why didn't you say something to us or to your parents?" I asked.

"I was too embarrassed and scared. Now I realized I should have told my parents," she confessed. I won't make that mistake again!"

Then her eyes welled up with tears again as she said, "Thank you so much for the book and for being here!"

"Where else would we be?" I said as we all hugged.

Just then, Sara came into Glenda's bedroom. She showed up with Glenda's homework.

"What did I miss, what did I miss?"

Glenda waved her toward the bed and said, "Come here and get in on this."

Sara ran over and jumped onto the bed, embraced our huddle and quietly said, "Haili." For the first time since Haili's death, we sobbed in each other's arms.

After a while, Glenda looked around and asked, "Where is Natalia? She was supposed to be here an hour ago."

Glenda recovered and returned to school after two weeks, just in time for graduation and all the festivities. The doctors and prayer saved Glenda's life, but we saved her spirit. We showed up with love and encouragement during and after her crisis. It's the smallest acts of kindness, an encouraging word, just showing up or standing beside someone in silence that can heal a broken heart or body. It has the power to change the direction or future of a person's life. As young as we were, we understood that. We were also now painfully aware of how fragile and short life can be. All we have is now and to cherish each other and every moment.

Chapter Twenty-One

GRADUATION DAY

I sat up in bed and woke up with a start! Gasping for breath, eyes wet, heart-pounding, perspiring! It happened again! The same dream! I am always lost and running through a dark neighborhood trying to find my way back home! This was a regular occurrence. I would have settled for the other dream I had before this one. It's the one where I am in school, with no clue as to where my classroom is or the answers to the test we are about to take.

I jumped in the shower with a million thoughts going through my head. Today would be a regular school morning, graduation ceremony, graduation luncheon, then dismissal by noon. We would then go to the luncheon/hootenanny in the Church Hall and afterwards to Robert's for our graduation swim party. My fourteenth birthday was the next day. The girls were coming over in the afternoon, then we would go to the studios to visit Cindy on the set of her movie and then, a sleepover at my house.

Then it happened. Too much water got into my mouth. My front right tooth cap came off and was circling the drain! It had broken off the day before as I bit into a T-bone steak. There had been no time to get it fixed. I was able to attach it back temporarily, but had to be careful not to let it fall out. I panicked as I tried to catch it. How could I go to graduation with just a stub for a front tooth?!

As I desperately tried to catch my cap, the memory of the car accident that caused my broken teeth four years earlier all came flooding back. My mom was going to California to be in my grandfather's on stage variety show. My mom's friend, Mary, offered to drive her to the airport and I went along for the ride. While we were waiting for her plane to take off, I noticed a family of five. They all had the biggest buck teeth I had ever seen. I was making fun of them in my mind and laughed to myself.

On the way home, Mary and I got into a head-on collision with another car. There were no seat belts back then. I flew into the dashboard. My right knee started to hurt. I could see the rain falling. Mary was unconscious or dead; I did not know for sure. Then, I noticed my broken teeth in the indented dashboard.

I spent years in dentist chairs and had to endure nine year old classmates making fun of me because the temporary teeth were silver. A girl named Agnes said I looked like a maniac in front of all the other kids. I thought that God was punishing me for making fun of the family with the buck teeth. I never made fun of anyone ever again and hated it when I saw people tease or make fun of others.

Got it! Caught it just before it went down the drain! I got dressed and went to our classroom, for the last time! Somehow, the room seemed much smaller. Haili's desk was covered with cards, pictures, flowers, and ribbons to be given to her family after the ceremony. I was relieved to see her desk filled with love tokens instead of an empty desk. I looked around at each face and made a mental note so I would always remember them. We all looked so pretty or handsome in our outfits. Some of the girls even wore makeup. We went to church and sang our songs, received our graduation certificates and Father Francis' blessing. Our families looked on with pride as we lined up for the graduation picture. None of us stayed very long at the luncheon/hootenanny because we all had better plans and couldn't wait to get to the swim party at Robert's house.

Robert's party started at 4 p.m. so Sara, Glenda, Patty and I decided to congregate at Jack's house for a few hours. My sister, Cindy, and her boyfriend, Rick, drove all of us girls to Jack's. Natalia, Barbara Jean and Jenny were already there. As usual, just the rebel boys Paul, Jack, Ronnie, Frank, and Preston showed up. Peter, Casey and some of the other boys from the class were all at Robert's house helping him set up for the party. They were preparing the track for the big Go Cart Races.

There were no parents or food at Jack's party. I don't think they knew we were even there; they were not home. Glenda and I started to sing and dance to the music when the boys suggested we all play spin the bottle. We were supposed to follow the rules and play, truth or dare and seven minutes in heaven, whatever that was. We all sat in a circle. Natalia was up first. As she leaned over to spin the bottle I could not believe my eyes! There it was! Hanging around her neck was the necklace that I saw in Jack's room on his night stand a few weeks earlier!

"What the hell?!" I screamed.

"My boyfriend and my best friend are going together and no one bothered to tell me?!"

Without taking her angry eyes off Natalia, Patty said, "Come on, Diane; let's go."

Glenda followed us outside and said, "Gosh, I'm so sorry Diane. I'll meet you guys at Robert's later. I need to go home and rest first."

As we walked down the winding street from Jack's house I thought about how quickly my life changed from "Happy Together" to "Kind of a Drag." The lyrics of those songs pretty much said what I was feeling.

I stopped walking, turned to Patty and said, "P, I can't believe it. I'm so bummed out and pissed I could spit nails!"

"Are you surprised?" Patty replied.

I was completely dumbfounded. Shaking my head and blinking a few times I asked, "What do mean? Did you know?"

Shrugging her shoulders she answered, "No, not exactly, but you know Natalia, she is usually out for herself."

I was beginning to see what Patty was trying to tell me. Natalia could be extremely opinionated and condescending at times. Her aloofness and self-centered attitude was difficult to be around sometimes. If you wanted to hang out with her, it pretty much had to be on her terms.

I had to sit down on the curb to catch my breath.

"I thought Natalia loved me!" I sobbed. "Shit, I love her more than Jack. I thought she felt the same way about me, but apparently not! We are friends and supposed to have each other's back!"

Patty put her hand on my shoulder, shook her head in agreement and said, "Yeah well, you can't expect people to feel about you or treat you the same way you do. If you do, you will always be disappointed! As far as Jack is concerned, he is a player. You didn't know that?"

I looked at her through swollen eyes and replied, "No, I didn't know that, not really! Well, maybe I did. I did wonder why he was acting so distant lately. Why didn't you tell me what you thought?" I asked angrily.

"Hey, Diane, don't take it out on me! Besides, would you have listened to me if I had told you?"

"Probably not, but next time tell me anyway!"

"Okay! Okay!" she promised. "But, be careful what you ask for."

"Why, what do you mean?" I asked.

"You always get mad when I tell you the truth, you need to toughen up!"

Then she held out her hand and said, "Come on now, Diane, get up and let's get going. It's getting late."

I was never really comfortable hitchhiking because I

did not trust strangers. I usually used my skateboard to get around. Patty hitched rides all the time, so I went along with it again. Everywhere you looked, especially on Sunset Strip, young people crowded the streets while they hitched rides between all the clubs and hung out.

This young couple with very long hair picked us up in their VW van. On the way, they invited us to go with them to a party as they offered us a hit from their joint. That's what it was like back then. Everyone was friendly and high or both. We were still too young to get into that scene so we declined the party and the joint. Besides, we were anxious to get to Robert's and it was getting late.

They dropped us off about two miles from Robert's house. Out go our thumbs and this time this mangy looking older guy with dirty hair and a long, dirty beard picked us up. I hesitated to go into his filthy car, but Patty was already in the front seat. I sat right behind her. He asked us a lot of questions while Patty conversed with him. I was silent and very uncomfortable. All of sudden, he pulled the car into an alleyway and stopped the car. I could see Patty's shoulders bobbing up and down. I knew she was laughing, but this time from nerves and fright. Without saying a word, we simultaneously bolted out of the car and ran like hell!

"P, could this day get any worse?" I screamed as I tried to catch up with her.

WE WALKED THE REST OF THE WAY AND GOT TO THE party two hours late, tired and perspired, but glad to be in one piece. I was certain I would never hitch a ride again.

Most of our classmates were already there when we arrived except for Jack and Natalia. Jenny had not arrived yet either. I was not sure what went on between her and Jack and hoped she would not show up at the party.

Tara, Ellie, and Peggy were helping with the set-up for dinner. Of all the kids in the class, they were the most devastated because Haili was their best friend. Barbara Jean was sitting on the couch by herself looking on with her arms crossed. She seemed upset as usual. No one asked her why for fear of being dragged into her next dramatic delusion.

Tara looked around and asked Patty, "What's the matter with Diane?"

"Yeah, she looks like she has been crying," Ellie added.

Still angry, Patty replied, "Diane and Jack broke up and it's all Natalia's fault!"

I had been in the bathroom washing my face while Sara helped me put some makeup on. When we came out of the bathroom, Glenda had just arrived. We all walked over to Patty and the rest of the girls. To my surprise they all started giving me hugs. As Peggy pulled away from her hug and said, "What a bummer Diane, we are so sorry!"

"Yeah, don't cry anymore!" Ellie added as Tara and Peggy shook their heads in agreement.

They were so reassuring and nice to me. I started to feel bad that I had been calling them "The Goodie Two

Shoes" all this time and that I never tried to get to know them better. I was a bit overwhelmed with their kindness. I started to cry again and said, "Thank you, you guys! Let's all try to keep in touch okay?" We all agreed.

I noticed that Barbara Jean was no longer sitting on the couch. As I looked around the house, I asked the kids, "Has anyone seen Barbara Jean?"

Pointing toward the door Tara replied, "She stormed off and went out into the side yard."

As I made my way to the side yard to find Barbara Jean, I recalled the time I spent the night at her house a few weeks back. We had just won the volleyball championship when Barbara Jean turned to Natalia and I and said, "Let's celebrate our victory. Come to my house tonight for a sleepover!"

Caught up in all the excitement, we both agreed. I figured if Natalia was there it wouldn't be so bad. I just did not feel comfortable around Barbara Jean to hang out with her on my own.

Her home was a mansion in Hollywood. It was amazingly and beautifully decorated in white décor. Everything looked immaculate. There was a magnificent, white baby grand piano in the living room and a white polar bear rug between the piano and the fireplace. I could not take my eyes off the bear's black, lifeless eyes. I wondered what compelled people to kill such magnificent creatures and why they displayed the carcasses like a trophy or prize. It made me sad. The energy in that house was sad. Her mom was not home and rarely was.

This was just a couple of weeks after I saw Jack and

Jenny talking that night I went on the car ride. I was still upset about that and most of all, at my parents for not showing up for the volleyball tournament. We won, and they missed it! As a result, I stupidly decided to get 14 shot glasses of liquor from different bottles at the bar. I drank them all down, one right after the other, becoming sick as a dog!

I was completely, disgustingly drunk. When she helped me put my pajamas on, I remembered how strange she stared at me, but then I passed out. The next morning I thought I was going to die. I was lucky I did not die from alcohol poisoning. We went to Sunday mass. I kept praying and vowed to God that I would never drink like that again if He would just help me stand up and not throw up again.

Ever since that night, Barbara Jean kept coming up to me. She would just appear out of nowhere. She always seemed to want to tell me something, but then, she would just rush off and disappear.

My mind came quickly back to the present when I found myself in the side yard facing Barbara Jean. There she was, sitting on the ground all alone, brooding with her head down and arms crossed. She glanced sideways at me. There was a long silence. I figured she was still mad at me because I had been avoiding her.

I was about to ask her what was wrong when she blurted out, "I always wanted to be friends with you, just you! No one wants me around because you all think I am a monster! You all look so happy and come from perfect homes. Unlike me, my family is sick and so am I. I may be pathetic and sad, but I am not a monster!"

"Wow, this is really heavy Barbara Jean!" I said. I sat down beside her and continued, "Why do you think you are sick?"

"Because I...I don't like boys…I think I only like girls!"

"I never realized you wanted to be THAT kind of a friend," I replied in shock. "Besides, you always seem to be mad at me and everyone else for that matter. Why didn't you say something?"

"I never had the courage until now. Something is wrong with me…Don't tell anyone," she pleaded.

"Don't worry, I won't, I promise! But....you know I like boys, right? Actually, I think I'm boy crazy!"

With a slight smile on her face she moved her hands from her eyes and started to rub her chin. I could tell she was thinking. I wasn't sure if she would listen to me or punch me. She was always so unpredictable. I took a chance and continued, "Listen Barbara Jean, first of all I want to apologize for getting so drunk at your house. I am sorry! I hope you will believe me when I say that none of us come from perfect homes. It may just seem that way, but trust me, we all struggle and have our secrets. I can tell you for sure, no one thinks you are a monster! The only one who thinks that is you!"

"But…"

"No buts!" I continued. "You are not pathetic and sad, stop saying that! If you say that enough times you will believe that and become that. We all make mistakes. Think of yourself in a good light. You are not your family. You are beautiful because God made you in His image and He does not make mistakes! He loves you and so do I. But, not like that...I mean just as friends okay? If you change the way you see yourself in a good positive way, others will see it as well!"

I stood up. This time, I was the one holding my hand down to someone to help them up, just like Patty did with me earlier that day.

"Come on now, get up! Let's go have some fun! Okay?"

"Okay!" she said. I think that may have been the first time I ever saw her smile.

ROBERT SECRETLY HAD A CRUSH ON ME, BUT NEVER told me until many years later. Maybe that's why he seemed a bit angry and dismissive with me. He must have been jealous because of Jack. He came from a wealthy family. Their large home was beautiful, nestled in the Hollywood Hills with the most amazing view I had ever seen. His Mother was very kind and absolutely beautiful. She looked like Carole Lombard.

One of her best friends was Mrs. Annatelli, Peter's mom. Both she and Peter looked alike because they wore the same glasses and had red hair. Peter's father owned an Italian restaurant. Whenever there was an event that involved the school or the kids, they were always there feeding us with the most delicious food. They were all so generous and kind.

As I was getting a plate of food, Mrs. Annatelli looked at my swollen eyes and said, "Never forget your friends because they will become more important to you as you grow older. Most importantly, always remember, in order to have true friends you must first be one!"

I wondered if she somehow knew about Natalia. Perhaps she overheard the girls and Patty talking about it. Was I not a true friend to Natalia? Did I somehow deserve what happened? No, I did not think so, but still, I was very confused. I wondered how I would ever speak to her again.

I went outside to enjoy the Go Cart races. It was winner keeps going. None of the girls dared to compete except me. I could never resist a challenge especially when the boys said girls can't participate. My inner tom boy emerged as I jumped in the Go Cart.

"What are you doing?" Robert protested.

Batting my eyes I replied, "Oh, come on, Robert, just let me drive this one race. I will probably have to concede when I lose."

"Well, okay," Robert agreed.

He was so sure of himself he did not start out on point. I breezed around the track without fear and beat him. Next up was Preston. All the boys were cheering for him on the sidelines and beating their chests like little cravens. The girls were jumping up and down like cheerleaders and Casey was actually standing next to them cheering me on as well.

Lined up with our Go Carts side by side, Preston shouted, "You are not going to beat me!"

"Watch me!" I laughed.

Preston was so determined to beat me that he became reckless and spun out of control and tipped over. Everyone ran up to him to see if he was all right.

As he limped away, we could see that he scrapped his leg and elbow. He was not badly hurt except maybe his ego. One by one, I beat them all. Far out, what a blast! Casey helped me up out of the Go Cart then gave me a hug and thumbs up.

It was still warm outside so I went inside and started to dance with all the girls and to my surprise, all the boys joined in. Preston had a huge crush on Glenda and stoically stared at her with his piercing blue eyes, like he always did. Patty poked my side, pointed at Preston and whispered, "Look at this!"

He slowly walked over and finally asked Glenda to dance. That was quite a leap for him since he never even had the courage to talk to her, ever! Preston was trying so hard to impress Glenda with his dance moves that he lost his balance and tripped over his own feet, falling to the ground. Frank quickly cut in and whisked her away. I never saw Glenda smile so much.

The sunset was a magnificent array of colors. Indigo blue, violet, powder blue, yellow, orange, and red with silhouetted Palm trees in the distance! I started to feel much better and decided to join the kids in the pool.

There was a sauna next to the pool so I went inside. The heat felt so good and I enjoyed the solitude even more. Robert appeared in the doorway. He had heard about Jack and Natalia and figured it was now or never. When he saw me sitting there, he closed the door behind him. Clark Kent left the building and Superman emerged! He swooped me up in his arms and planted the most passionate, intense kiss on me ever! His kiss was so aggressive that our teeth knocked pretty hard. He must have been storing up the courage to kiss me all year! Locked in our kiss, he suddenly pulled back and looked like he was chewing on something. I realized it was my tooth's cap!

"Don't swallow it!!!" I screamed.

Stunned, he pulled it out of his mouth and handed it to me. I attempted to hook it back over my tooth. Oh sweet Mother of God! I wanted to die! Disappear! I ran out of the sauna, jumped in the water and swam to the other side of the pool. Robert burst out from the sauna and yelled, "Gosh Diane, I'm so sorry!"

I was now standing in the shallow end of the pool embarrassed and completely mortified. I knew the kids were all wondering what had happened in the sauna. But, I realized that when I jumped into the pool that stupid cap came off again!

I started yelling to all the kids in the pool, "Wait! Wait! Don't move! Help me find my cap! Robert, Preston, and Peter gingerly swam and scoured the bottom of the pool for at least ten minutes. It seemed like a lifetime had passed when Peter swam to the top with a big smile and proudly handed me my cap. They had all seen me with my stubbed tooth and somehow, it didn't even matter to them. These guys were my friends!

Chapter Twenty-Two

BIRTHDAY SURPRISE

The next morning, I woke up to my girlfriends bursting into my room, before they dragged me out of bed. It was the tradition to kidnap a friend on their birthday. The rule was to not let the victim shower, dress, brush teeth, or even go to the bathroom. We piled into Natalia's mom's car and were dropped off at IHOP for breakfast. Apparently, the girls had planned this birthday surprise way before graduation day and decided to go through with it. After we were seated, Patty, Glenda, and Sara watched as Natalia and I hashed it out.

"Where's the necklace?" I demanded.

"I gave it back to Jack and broke it off," she replied in her usual dismissive manner.

I pounded my fist on the table.

"It? What was it? How long were you seeing him behind my back?" I seethed.

She rolled her eyes and flatly stated, "Look, it's over! Besides, I never really cared for him that much anyway."

"Really? Are you kidding me? So you broke my heart for the hell of it?"

"Not everything is about you, Diane!" she snapped.

I stood up from the table flailing my Italian hands in the air. "What? Is your mind bent? He was my boyfriend and you knew it! If you honestly cared for him it would make it easier to forgive, just like King Arthur did in Camelot. But, you're not even sorry!"

She thought for a moment and replied, "This isn't a movie, Diane. It's not that simple."

I sat back down at the table and demanded, "Okay then, explain it to me!"

"Well…um… I'm sorry you were hurt, but I still don't think I did anything wrong. Jack told me you guys were broken up."

"And you believed him? You should have asked me!" I replied as I beat my chest.

Patty chimed in and pointed her finger in Natalia's face and declared, "Bullshit, Natalia! You knew Diane thought Jack was still her boyfriend. Besides, even if they were broken up, it's not cool to date your girlfriend's ex-boyfriends!"

Leaning back in her seat with arms extended out toward us, Natalia replied, "Back off man, both of you! Chill out or I'm out of here!"

At this point the entire restaurant was engaged in our explosive conversation. When we noticed this, we all became silent for what seemed a lifetime. Finally, Natalia spoke up. "So, do you want to end our friendship? Should I get up and walk away?"

"Walk away? You don't get it, do you?" I replied.

"Get what?" she asked.

"What unconditional love is. Yes, I am furious at you. I don't know why I still want you in my life after what you have done, but I do. I think anger, fear, love, and hatred are feelings we all have from time to time, especially with family and friends. My mom did not have any siblings so her friends became her sisters, her family. And, that is what you are to me, family. So, I don't want you to go anywhere."

I did not want to lose Natalia as a friend. Jack was not worth it, but for some reason, I believed she was, and deserved a second chance. I realized that fighting over a boy and Natalia's betrayal didn't seem as important in light of Haili's death. There were bigger things to consider — the war, struggles at home, and figuring out who we were. They say that teenagers only think of themselves, but I was learning to consider the world around me.

FROM THE PANCAKE HOUSE WE WALKED FOR MILES back to my house. We had to get showered and dressed to go to the studios to see my sister's movie set. She was also going to treat us to my birthday dinner at the commissary. On the way, we stopped at Fosters Freeze. I loved the vanilla ice cream dipped in chocolate. I don't know what came over me, but I could not resist the urge to give Natalia an ice cream facial with chocolate sprinkles and a cherry on top! Some of it got on Glenda.

"My hair!!" she screamed.

Glenda, in turn, flung her ice cream at me and all hell broke out! Before we knew it, there was ice cream everywhere! All five of us engaged in the best food fight ever! Our screams of anger soon turned into laughter, tears, and hugs! The immigrant Foster Freeze owner yelled at us, "You girls crazy! You go home now! I call police!"

We hightailed it out of there and headed back to my house.

We got cleaned up in a hurry, just in time to pile into my dad's car. My mom, Cindy, and Gino were already at the studio waiting for her to shoot her last scene for the day. The movie my sister starred in was called "Impossible Years." David Niven played her father. We toured the set and met all the stars of the show. I had never seen a movie set before. The movie set house was completely built and furnished. It also had a real swimming pool.

Then we went to the set of "Lost in Space!" I could not believe that the rocks that looked so large and real on TV were actually very light and small. It was all quite exciting for all of us, especially for my little brother, Gino. We waited for the cast to complete their scenes and then we got to meet them.

After the tour, we made our way to the commissary for dinner. I wondered why the commissary door was so huge. Cindy knocked and made sure that all five of us were standing side by side. When the door opened, we absolutely lost our minds!

"Is that the…MonkeeMobile?" Sara asked as she jumped up and down clapping her hands.

"Wait! What?!" Glenda screamed while she fluffed up her hair.

"Is this the set of The Monkees?" Patty squealed.

Then, Davy, Micky, Michael, and Peter came out from back stage to greet us!

Cindy grabbed Sara's camera and started taking pictures of all of us.

I thought Patty was going to faint when Davy put his arm around her to take a picture. For as long as I could remember I wanted to bring some happiness to Patty. This definitely did the trick. Watching her giggle and laugh actually brought me more joy than I had ever experienced.

Cindy turned to me and said, "Happy Birthday Di Di."

I could hardly contain myself. "I had no idea they were even here and that you knew them! Oh my God! Far out! Thank you!"

That birthday, I learned the profound lesson that Cindy did take notice of me and cared enough to help me and my girlfriends' dream come true. That's why even though we were finally meeting and being surrounded by our favorite rock stars, I could not take my eyes off my sister!

THAT NIGHT WE WERE SO EXCITED FROM THE EVENTS of the day that we could not sleep. Each of us had our own reasons to search for the band. We did not realize it at the time that what we were searching for was ourselves. To figure out who we were and what we were going to do with the rest of our lives.

It was 1 a.m. in the morning when we all snuck out from my house and walked around the block. We did not care that we just had our baby doll nighties on. We had no fear of predators. We were just in the moment. The night was balmy with a slight breeze blowing in our hair. The stars and moon lit up the night sky. It was glorious! There we were, five friends enjoying the elements and each other. We were young, beautiful, invincible, and grateful it was all ahead of us -- our wonderful life and future!

EPILOGUE

As the music plays on in my head and the memories of the past surround me, I returned to the present. Waiting for "P" to call me back, I found myself in my car hugging the curves of Laurel Canyon – the streets I had frequented so many times before. I started to sing aloud. "I thought love was only true in fairy tales..."

I LEARNED MANY LIFE LESSONS THAT YEAR FROM 1966 to 1967...

- Love starts with God. He is not so far off into the distance. I could actually talk to Him and feel His presence when I was open to hearing His voice. He has His reasons for allowing certain things to happen. Even if we don't agree or understand, we must always trust Him.

- Everything I needed was right in front of me. If you miss it, you will stay lost. Reaching out to others helped me see that. Sometimes, you just have to get out of your own way.
- Love was not about finding a Knight in Shining Armor.
- Judging others without truly knowing them is a mistake.
- I was important to my family after all.
- Having friends and being a friend is a treasured gift.

I would be remiss if I did not say that all the kids in the class left an indelible mark on me and on each other. Some were good, some were bad, but mostly good. I guess it depends on one's perspective. For me, eighth grade was the best time I ever had in school and that was because of my classmates. Even though I did not call them all out by name, I will never forget them.

And as I wrote about that last day in the classroom, I remember and miss each and every one of them still 50 years later. We were all insecure, scared pre-teens. We spent a lot of time together in the classroom, playground, church, and each other's homes. We laughed, cried, fought, encouraged, and loved one other.

Most of us went our separate ways. The transience of childhood and the friends we make is inevitable. We became spouses, mothers, fathers, grandparents, and professionals. But no matter how independent we thought we were, there was something that always tied us together. And, sometimes, if lucky and blessed, you take away a few lifelong friends.

Life is beautiful with many blessings and moments to experience and enjoy. We will, however, have difficult and sometimes unbearable trials. Rejoice, because it is during those times that we will grow the most when we trust in God to get us through it. We must focus on our blessings with grateful hearts and not on the negative.

Everything that has happened in our lives is for a reason and a purpose. No matter what happens in life, we have a choice to become "Bitter or Better."

I chose Better!

REFERENCES

- Saint Theresa of Lisieux, 1873-1897; "Our Lord does not look so much at the greatness of our actions or even at their difficulty, as at the Love with which we do them."
- Martin Luther King Jr., August 28, 1963; "I have a dream that one day this nation will rise up and live out the true meaning of its creed: 'We hold these truths to be self-evident: that all men are created equal.'"

The Bible NIV

- First Timothy 2:5 "For there is one God and one mediator between God and men, the man Christ Jesus."
- Philippians 4:6-7 "Do not be anxious about

anything, but in everything, by prayer and petition, with thanksgiving, present your request to God and the peace of God, which transcends all understanding, will guard your hearts and your minds in Christ Jesus.'"

- Romans 10:9-10 "Because if you confess with your mouth that Jesus is Lord and believe in your heart that God raised him from the dead, you will be saved. For with the heart one believes and is justified, and with the mouth one confesses and is saved.'"
- Ephesians 2:8-9 "For it is by grace you have been saved, through faith, and this not from yourselves, it is a gift of God – not by works, so that no one can boast."

The Bible ESV

Ecclesiastes 3:1-8

- 1. To everything there is a season, and a time to every purpose under the heaven:
- 2. a time to be born, and a time to die; a time to plant, and a time to pluck up that which is planted;
- 3. a time to kill, and a time to heal; a time to break down, and a time to build up;
- 4. a time to weep, and a time to laugh; a time to mourn, and a time to dance;
- 5. a time to cast away stones, and a time to

gather stones together; a time to embrace, and a time to refrain from embracing;

- 6. a time to seek, and a time to lose; a time to keep, and a time to cast away;
- 7. a time to tear, and a time to sew; a time to keep silence, and a time to speak;
- 8. a time to love, and a time to hate; a time of war, and a time of peace.

- 1 Thessalonians 4:13-14 "Brothers and sisters, we do not want you to be uninformed about those who sleep in death, so that you do not grieve like the rest of mankind, who have no hope.
- For we believe that Jesus died and rose again, and so we believe that God will bring with Jesus those who have fallen asleep in Him."

Dear Reader…

Thank you for taking time to read, "Looking for Davy Jones." If you enjoyed it, please consider telling your friends or posting a short review. Word of mouth is an author's best friend and much appreciated.

— *Diana Ferrare-Magaldi*

ACKNOWLEDGMENTS

First and foremost, I'd like to thank my Lord and Savior Jesus Christ for His saving grace, love, and tremendous blessings. Through Him all things are possible.

My husband, Dennis, love of my life. Danielle, my daughter and soul sister. Thank you for your unwavering love, support, and encouragement. To all my children, stepchildren, grandchildren, siblings, nieces, and nephews, I love you all beyond the moon and stars!

Margery Walshaw, whose incredible talent and expertise helped me with editing and formatting of the book.

Michael, Kylie, Danielle, Katherine, Cristina, Gino, Nancy, and Dennis for reading the first draft and giving me invaluable feedback.

Patty, Glenda, Robert, and Preston for sharing some of your memories, feedback, and most of all, thank you for your support and friendship all these years.

Patty and Glenda for sitting and listening to chapter after chapter during the writing process even when you did not want to.

ABOUT THE AUTHOR

Diana Ferrare-Magaldi places many titles upon herself including author, wife, mother, grandmother, and loyal friend. She is also a devout Christian and Cancer survivor.

In addition to writing, she enjoys a 20 plus year career as a real estate agent, specializing in the Conejo Valley of California where she and her husband reside.

Her debut novel, "Looking for Davy Jones," is a coming-of-age tale about five teenage girls growing up in the turbulent 1960s amidst the backdrop of the Vietnam War, flower children, rock and roll, and the Civil Rights movement. She draws inspiration from her favorite authors including Joseph Campbell, Philippa Gregory, Ken Follett, Michael Connelly, Diana Gabaldon, and George R.R. Martin.

When not writing, Diana paints with oils and is an accomplished cook. She combines these passions into her writing and has plans for a cookbook and an inspirational novel.

Made in the USA
San Bernardino, CA
25 June 2018